Before the Christmas Wedding

Giselle Lumas

Before the Christmas Wedding

By Giselle Lumas

This is a work of fiction. Names, characters, businesses, events, and incidents are the products of the author's imagination. Any resemblance to actual persons, living or dead, or actual events is purely coincidental.

For Mom.

I love you and miss you.

Chapter One

"How could they be so unbelievably selfish?! I mean, what the actual f—" Amanda Alexander said after she pressed the red disconnect button on her cell phone.

"Before you finish that sentence, need I remind you, you just randomly gave up cursing not more than ten minutes ago," Dexter Richardson pointed out to his neighbor before crawling back under her sink.

"Fudgsicles and popsicle sticks!" Amanda shouted instead of the colorful four-letter word she wanted to scream.

"That's better." Dexter's voice was now muffled from the sink. "Can you pass me the flashlight?"

Amanda absentmindedly grabbed the light and passed it to him.

"Thanks," he said before grunting. He tinkered a bit, then urged, "So, explain what's got you so upset?"

"That was Rachel. You know, William's girlfriend. They got engaged last night, and they want to hire me as their wedding planner."

"Wow, that's amazing! You'll get a lot of exposure from their wedding. Rachel knows a lot of people. Not to mention her mom is famous." Not only was Rachel a well-known and respected real estate agent, but her mother was Desire Collins—a mega soap opera star back in the day and a current super movie star who appeared in too many blockbuster hits to count or name.

"A Christmas wedding . . . as in three months from now. How do they expect me to pull that off? How? How could they do this to me?" Amanda felt the pressure building in her throat. She knew it had nothing to do with the time crunch. She'd been able to pull a wedding off in just a few short weeks. Her displeasure, sadness, and grief were over the groom, William (aka her crush since she was eight).

William was her brother's lifelong best friend. She was almost sure both her brother and William knew how Amanda felt. There was no way for them not to know. She'd written about him so many times in her diary, and she'd caught them numerous times reading it. It was humiliating. Why would William torture her this way by asking her to plan their wedding? And to Rachel of all people!

"He knows you're struggling with your business but believes in your work. He's trying to help you," Dex reasoned as he tinkered with the plumbing.

She snorted, then flat-out denied it. "I am not struggling."

"Right . . . When you aren't busy planning a wedding, you're doing food deliveries; if not, you provide childcare after school and sometimes during random weekends. That's not struggling? At some point, you'll need a break, or *you* will break."

"It's not struggling. It's called hustling. I'm fine. I need to keep busy. I don't like to be idle."

"Keep telling yourself that, kid."

She stomped her foot. "I'm not a kid."

This time he snorted, then laughed. He scooted himself out from underneath the sink and announced proudly, "That should do it. I'll turn the water back on, and there should be no more leaks."

"Thanks, Dex."

"Anytime, Manz."

She grinned at his nickname for her. Ever since they became next-door neighbors a few years ago, he'd called her that. No one else called her by that name. It made her feel special.

"I'll be going out to a friend's house to watch the game later. If you need anything, just text me."

"Okay. Thank you for fixing the sink."

"You're welcome." He went outside, then returned to the kitchen a few minutes later. "Just to make sure, turn the water on." Amanda did as requested. The water sputtered briefly, then came out smoothly. Dex checked the bottom of the sink. "Great! Good as new. No leak."

"Have fun at your friend's house."

He gathered up the rest of his tools and said, "I will. See you later." He was out the door.

Amanda glanced around the small house she inherited from her grandmother. It was a two-bedroom house with a family room, kitchen, and one full bathroom. She had a washer and dryer in her one-car garage. It was all paid for. The home had its issues, but it was hers. She only had to walk half a block, and she'd be on the beach. Beach City, California, was her hometown. She never wanted to live anywhere else.

Her grandmother used to be big on sewing, knitting, and crocheting. She had homemade blankets and quilts scattered about the house, and little ceramic trinkets on small, random shelves and in a glass display case. Amanda vowed never to get rid of them. They reminded her of her grandmother. She missed her so much. It had been three years since she passed, but it still felt like yesterday or only a few hours ago. Her grandmother had been one of her best friends. They would talk for hours about wedding ideas. They loved to decorate and watch people be amazed by their creations. They also enjoyed planning parties and standing back to watch how people enjoyed themselves.

"Oh, Grandma, I wish you were here. You'd tell me how to plan this wedding," she whispered, and grabbed one of the crocheted throw pillows from the white leather couch.

Christmas wedding, she thought, *colors would have to be red, green, gold, white, and silver. The invitations with doves and ribbon. Red or gold ink.* She frowned. *It could also be an ice wedding. Rachel was a bully. How could he marry her?*

"Ugh!" she shouted. "Focus. Let go of the past. Think . . ." She hand-made the invitations. It was one of the things that made her so popular and one that she was proud of. As long as the guest list was under a hundred, she could manage it. She knew she could count on her niece and Dex to help her out, saving her money and time. She pulled out her organizer and started her usual list of things to do for planning a wedding. She flipped through her calendar pages to pencil in tentative dates for events like wedding dress shopping, flowers, cake tasting, bachelorette and bachelor parties, etc. She knew her brother or one of his employees would most likely take the photos since he owned and operated a photography studio and was considered one of the best in Beach City.

She'd most likely try to book the wedding at DW Embassy Suites. It seemed to be the venue of choice in the winter. The problem was it might already be booked for one of the many corporate holiday parties. She'd have to check as soon as possible. She could also check if the park was available. It was another popular spot. They could have the ceremony right on the bridge above the pond if the weather permitted. The guests could sit below while the bride and groom exchanged vows on top, right smack in the middle of the bridge.

Amanda felt her throat swell up from unshed tears. Her light-brown eyes were misting. "Stupid William," she said with a scowl and sniffed. "Clueless, stupid, dumb, funny, cute, and nice-ass William. Damn it." She covered her mouth when she realized she cursed out loud. "Stupid."

As Dex drove his white Jeep Gladiator heading toward his friend's house, he thought of Amanda. Her curly hair and the freckles scattered across her nose, which had been turning pink. He knew as soon as she had closed and locked the door behind him, she would cry. Seeing her distraught over some guy made his stomach feel uneasy. It brought up too many wounds that he didn't want to examine. But there he was, thoughts of his ex-wife playing across his mind. He felt anger bubble up to the surface.

Erika Jenkins had nearly been the death of him. He'd fallen head over heels with her and her newborn son, Jeffrey. She'd reeled him in with her sad eyes and tears. She'd been mourning over her son's father. He wasn't dead but had been sent to prison for life for a murder she believed he didn't commit. A little alarm had rung in the back of his mind, but he ignored it. Erika's beauty enraptured Dex. She could have been a supermodel with green eyes, olive skin, and thick, dark hair. She'd been adopted, so she never knew her ethnicity. It didn't matter. Erika was beautiful inside and out. Or at least that was what he thought. They'd married after a few months of dating. They'd eloped in Vegas and started to build their life together in Phoenix, Arizona.

They'd been married for ten blissful months when things started to unravel quickly. She'd gotten a call one day, and it was as if a switch had been turned off. She began to distance herself. She wouldn't let him hold her. He couldn't kiss her. A few weeks later, he'd come home to find all of her and Jeffrey's things gone. He tried to call her, but she wouldn't answer. He'd finally received an email from her one night. Jeffrey's father had been released from prison on a technicality. She was getting back together with him and would be filing for divorce. Dex went numb.

A few days later, he'd been at a construction site he was managing when a tall, muscular man with broad shoulders, dark eyes, and a mean expression that must have reflected his soul approached him. "Dexter Richardson?"

He hadn't responded, but stood there in the dirt lot with the clipboard in his hand and wondered how fast he could get to his car before this guy caught up to him. His mind told him to run, but his body couldn't move.

"I'm Jeff. Thank you for looking after Erika and Junior." The man didn't appear to be thankful. Dexter swallowed, amazed that any part of him could function. Dex could only see and feel the evil radiate off this man. “You won’t be needed anymore. Stay away from them.” Jeff’s eyes threatened every fiber of Dex’s being.

Dex had been so rattled by the experience he left Arizona behind and moved to stay with his sister for a few months in Palm Hills, California. While he stayed with her, he watched his nieces and nephews. He enrolled in a real estate course. He earned his license and eventually found his own current home in Beach City. Dex planned to live as a hermit. He was sticking to the plan just fine until Amanda moved in next door three years ago.

Dexter felt the heat even today as he was driving. His cheeks felt flushed from the mixture of thoughts of Amanda and Erika. He felt so small. How could Erika love a man like Jeff? How could she pick Jeff over him? He clenched his teeth and gripped the steering wheel tighter.

“Nope, not falling for it,” he said to himself bitterly. He wasn’t going to lose his head and heart for the damsel in distress this time around.

Chapter Two

On Friday, which was the second weekend of October, Rachel informed Amanda there would be an engagement announcement dinner and demanded she attend. Amanda tried several times to decline the invitation politely, but William insisted, according to Rachel. "He says you're like his little sister, and he can't imagine such an important night happening without you present. Also, since you're the chosen wedding planner, it's pertinent that you be there."

"No, not really. I don't attend the engagement parties or anything. I just help plan them."

"He wants you there," Rachel insisted.

No! My heart can't take it. Why was he doing this to her? He knew she had a crush on him. Her brother knew. Her entire family knew. Why was he doing this?

"Please, Mandy," Rachel said, almost sounding desperate on the phone.

"Mandy? No one calls me Mandy. Call me Amanda, please." Amanda clenched her teeth. She knew she had no reason not to like Rachel. At least, not yet. Rachel just happened to be best friends with Caroline Winters. Caroline had bullied Amanda all through her junior high and high school years. Amanda supposed she did have some resentment toward Rachel for not stopping Caroline's torment. By default, Rachel was always a bully in Amanda's mind. She was guilty by association and lack of action. The reality was Amanda honestly didn't know the woman who had stolen her lifelong crush away from her. She had to give Rachel a chance. It was the right thing to do, not to mention professional, right? She had to terminate the thoughts of sneaking into Rachel's apartment and filling her shampoo bottle with liquid hair removal. She had to strangle the image of keying her freshly polished silver BMW. *Lord, forgive me for these thoughts.* She made the sign of the cross.

"Amanda, right. Sorry. I remember when you would come to the football games and have your hair in pigtails. Your brother called you Mandy back then, right?"

"Ugh." Amanda's shoulders slumped. "Yes, he did. I just never liked the nickname. I was bullied by a girl who used to call me that—long story. Just please, stick to Amanda. Thanks." The short version of the story was that she was overweight during her entire childhood until high school. Caroline repeatedly tormented her with the chant, "Mandy eats candy!" and her cackling laugh. She had even gone so far as throwing Tootsie Rolls and other candy at her. It was humiliating. She was grateful to the nutrition class and her PE teacher in high school, who talked and worked with her on healthy eating habits and lifestyle.

"Okay, so Amanda, will you please come to dinner tomorrow night? You're welcome to bring a date if you'd like. The food and drinks are on us. We haven't told anyone about the engagement: only you and our parents. So, please don't mention anything. We want to make a grand announcement during the dinner."

She breathed a heavy sigh and said, "Fine."

"Great! Meet us at Paul's Italian Pizzeria at seven thirty tomorrow night."

"See you then," Amanda said before clicking off her phone. She immediately dialed Dex's number. "Dex, will you come with me to dinner tomorrow? It's free food and drinks."

"Free is for me." He chuckled. "Just tell me where and what time."

"Paul's Italian at seven thirty tomorrow. I'll drive."

"Nah, we'll Uber. That way, we both can drink."

She laughed. "Deal."

Amanda and Dex promptly entered Paul's Italian Pizzeria on Saturday night at seven thirty. It was more crowded than usual. Half of the restaurant was sectioned off. Rachel immediately embraced Amanda in an unexpected tight hug. "My uncle owns the restaurant. He guessed why we wanted to have dinner here and invited more than anticipated. Sorry."

"No need to apologize. This is your party, not mine."

"Right," Rachel said.

Amanda thought Rachel looked a little flushed. "Are you okay?"

"Just a little overwhelmed. I'm so happy that we have you to help plan this wedding. I have no idea what I'm doing. I hate parties. I just . . . I would rather elope and not have a big to-do. My mom already talked to the pastor at Saint Michael's. He's agreed to meet with William and me twice a week for the premarital classes. It normally takes six months, but my mom pulled strings, being who she is. I'm sure the church will get a substantial donation. I'd just go to the courthouse or Vegas if it were up to me, but . . ." Rachel was talking fast, and her voice sounded shaky, but she paused to take a deep inhale and then slowly exhaled.

Amanda was surprised by Rachel's admission and behavior. She knew Caroline was constantly throwing parties. Amanda felt her heart soften a tiny bit toward Rachel. "It will be one of the best days of your life. I promise."

"She pulls off some amazing weddings," Dex said while approaching Amanda.

She felt his strong body press up behind her briefly and felt an odd stirring inside her. She'd never felt that before. Sure, she had butterflies before for William but what she was experiencing with Dex was completely different. She took a few deep breaths and did her best to ignore the feeling. It was probably stress and the overwhelming thoughts of losing her lifelong crush forever.

"Well, let me show you where you'll be sitting. I hope you don't mind sitting next to your brother."

"Why would you place me next to Matt?" Amanda joked as she and Dex made their way to the end of the long table where her brother sat. They each took a seat.

"Hey, dork, how've you been?" Matt asked, nudging his shoulder against hers before taking a sip of his ice water.

"I've been good, butthead. What about you?" Amanda asked, nudging him back.

"I'm doing okay, Mandy."

"Damn it, stop calling me Mandy!" Amanda whined.

"Manz, chill," Dex said in a whisper. "Cursing, remember?"

She groaned, then swatted at her brother's arm but said to Dex, "You don't have an annoying brother, so you would never understand."

Matt chuckled.

Dex rubbed Amanda's back in gentle circles. She leaned back into his caress and calmed down. *Mmmm*, she thought. *Dex's touch feels nice.* Her shoulders relaxed. He moved up to the back of her neck and gently gave her a one-handed massage. *God, he's impressive. Just one hand . . . what can he do with two?* Her eyes widened. She had no clue where that thought came from. She felt herself tense up again. Dex was in tune with her tension and began to knead knots out with his thumb. She began to relax again. *Mmmm.*

"So, where are your kids?" Amanda asked Matt. "Who's watching my awesome mini-me niece and adorable nephew?" Matt's daughter, Lexi, had the same shade of light-brown curly hair with golden highlights that went past her waist, light-brown eyes, and a sprinkle of freckles across the bridge of her nose and cheeks, just like Amanda. People would often mistake Amanda for Lexi's mother.

"One of the kids across the street from us," Matt explained. "We figured we can call this our date night." He gestured to his wife, Kimberly. Kimberly was engaged in an in-depth conversation with Rachel.

"They were on the cheer squad together back in the day, right?" Amanda asked.

"Yep, they were tight in high school. They kind of drifted apart when they each went away to college. But since Rachel started dating Willy, they seem to be close again."

"That's cool," Amanda said nonchalantly.

"So, are you okay with all of this?" Matt whispered so only she could hear the question.

"What do you mean?"

"I know you've had a crush on him forever. You okay with planning the wedding?"

"You already know about the wedding?"

"Of course. I helped Will pick out the engagement ring."

"Oh, right. You're his best friend, so you'll be the best man, right?"

"Of course." Matt nodded, then continued, "And one of the guys from my studio will be taking care of the photos." His dark-brown curly hair was cut short. His dark-brown eyes had sincere concern in them. "Seriously, sis, you okay with this?"

She swallowed, then shrugged her shoulders. "I don't have a choice," she whispered.

"I'm here for her," Dex said with soothing confidence. "We always have each other's backs, right, Manz?"

Amanda sniffed but said in a whisper, "Right."

Dex studied Amanda as she interacted with William throughout the evening. Her hands shook frequently. She flushed every once in a while. It was obvious she still had feelings for the man. She'd stiffen up whenever Rachel was within close proximity. He noticed she seemed a bit antsy around a woman named Caroline. Dex learned that Caroline was Rachel's best friend. He'd have to ask Amanda about her at some point.

He observed William too, and frowned. William was the kind of guy women would probably call *dreamy*. Dex rolled his dark-brown eyes from the thought. William looked like a cross between Brad Pitt and Patrick Dempsey with a strong jawline, hazel eyes, wavy light-brown hair, and a perfect smile. He tended to wear suits since he was a corporate attorney. His name was William, for crying out loud. Dex groaned audibly. How was he going to compete with that?

He paused his thinking. *Compete?* He wasn't competing for anything. Nope. He had no intentions of falling for the hyper, curly-haired, brown-eyed woman who had somehow become one of his best friends. Why would he? He didn't want to mess up their friendship. Nope. It was not happening.

Chapter Three

Almost a week later, it was the evening of the third Friday of October. Amanda and Rachel met in front of a small boutique on Main Street. Amanda was in jeans, white canvas shoes, and a pink tank top with her curly hair piled on her head in a messy bun. Rachel, however, was in a navy-blue dress suit with white pumps. Her straight blonde hair was down and perfect. No strands sticking out anywhere. Her makeup was flawless and done so that her blue eyes appeared to be bigger and more beautiful than ever. She seemed to be the same height as Amanda with her three-inch heels. Amanda was five-ten.

Rachel immediately embraced Amanda. "Thank you for meeting me here."

"You're welcome," Amanda said. "Most of my clients usually take their friends or family with them dress shopping. I set up the appointment for them, but I don't usually go."

"I'm sorry. I just wanted someone I could trust and have a real conversation with," Rachel said in a low voice.

Amanda tilted her head curiously. *How odd.* “What about Caroline or Kimberly? Or your mom?”

“Caroline and I aren’t that close anymore. She’ll be in the wedding, of course, but she tends to make everything about her. Kimberly is busy with her family. I don’t want to impose on her. My mom won’t like anything I pick out. We have completely different tastes and styles. I just want to find a dress and be done with it.”

Amanda blinked. “Oh,” was all she could think to say. She was beginning to wonder if Rachel wanted to get married. Amanda picked up a lot of negative energy from her. She couldn’t recall a moment when Rachel smiled or said something positive about getting married.

“This should be quick. I came in here a few days ago and saw something I liked, but I wanted to have another opinion before I purchase it. All sales are final here, so I just want to make sure.”

“Okay,” Amanda said. Rachel reached for Amanda’s right hand and tugged her into the store. The shop had different clothes, but a small section held unique, one-of-a-kind evening gowns. There were a few white gowns on the rack. Rachel shifted through a few dresses and then pulled out a white satin dress with a halter top and exposed back.

There were beads along the neckline and the bodice that pointed down toward the belly button.

Amanda frowned; not sure a halter dress would be fitting for someone like Rachel. She imagined Rachel in a full dress with ridiculous tulle, lace, and flowers. "Just have a seat over there. I'll be right out, okay?" Rachel said anxiously. She pointed Amanda to a chair near floor-length folding mirrors.

"Okay," Amanda said cautiously. She couldn't help but feel doubtful.

Rachel came out a few minutes later, and Amanda's mouth fell open from shock. The dress was stunning on her. It flattered her hourglass figure. It was formfitting and floor length, but when she turned, there was a sexy slit that exposed her right leg up to her thigh, giving a tiny glimpse of her hip. The back had a removable train that she could take off during the reception when she wanted to dance. "Wow!" That was all Amanda could say.

"Are you sure? I thought I would have to try on multiple dresses. This was only the second one I tried on, but I felt it was right."

"Oh yes!"

Rachel clapped her hands joyfully and then put her hands to her mouth. Her eyes glimmered with unshed tears. "I can't believe this is happening. I can't believe I'm marrying William."

"I can't either," Amanda said in a pained whisper.

"Are you okay?" Rachel asked, looking at Amanda in the mirror.

"Um . . . yeah. I mean, why wouldn't I be?"

"Your brother mentioned you used to have a crush on William. Are you over him, or are you still holding on to him somehow?"

Amanda studied Rachel momentarily. The question didn't sound cruel, not strictly concerned either, but it appeared to be a straightforward inquiry. Amanda cleared her throat and then tried to be as honest as possible. "I admit to having a crush on him when I was younger. I've grown a lot since then. You two are allowing me to promote my event planning company in a big way, so for that I will be eternally grateful."

Rachel tilted her head. "But you didn't answer the question." Rachel's happiness had disappeared from her face. A more serious and sterner look was in its place.

"Does it matter what my answer or any other woman's answer to that question would be? Willy asked *you* to marry him. Not me or any other woman. You. You said yes. I am a God-fearing and God-loving woman. I would never do anything to interfere with other relationships. Don't worry about what other women think. Only worry about what you and William think as a unit. Communicate with him. Trust him."

Rachel sighed and then glanced at her engagement ring.

"He chose you. My feelings don't matter," Amanda reassured her. Amanda was finding it difficult to breathe as a she felt the lump form in her throat from unshed tears.

Rachel's lips curved a tiny bit into a smile. She lifted her head again and looked at Amanda's reflection in the mirror. "You're right. Thank you, Amanda. You should be a politician. I know this is hard for you, but thank you from the bottom of my heart."

Amanda sniffed. "You're welcome."

"I have a dress to buy. Let me get out of this, pay for it, then I'll treat you to dinner."

"Oh, that won't be necessary," Amanda said. She was trying to think of an excuse to go home, but nothing would come to mind.

While Rachel was in the dressing room changing, Amanda sent Dex a text.

Dex, call me. Tell me there is an emergency or something.

She waited a few seconds. When there was no response, she called him. When his voice mail picked up, she said loud enough she was sure Rachel could hear her, “Oh, hey, Dex. I almost missed your call. My phone was on vibrate. What’s up?” Amanda paused then said, “Uh-huh . . . Oh . . . Oh no, that’s horrible. Yes, of course I’ll go with you. We just finished here. I’ll meet you there in ten.”

When Rachel walked out of the dressing room, Amanda said, “I’m sorry, Rachel. I’ll have to take a rain check on the dinner. I have to meet Dex. He’s having some sort of issue somewhere, and I have to go um . . . meet him at the . . . at . . . somewhere.”

Rachel looked at Amanda inquisitively but said, “Sure, right. Okay. Another time. Thank you again, Amanda. Drive safe.”

“Thanks,” Amanda said as she quickly backed out of the store and then rushed to her car.

Chapter Four

Dex appeared on Amanda's doorstep the following morning with a bag of doughnuts and two coffees. She opened the door wide to allow him in. "So, explain the voice mail," Dex said, handing her a coffee.

"Where were you?" Amanda asked.

"I was wrapping up a property sale. It takes a while," Dex explained. "Now, explain the cryptic message."

"I went with Rachel while she tried on a dress, and she wanted to take me to dinner. I needed an out," she explained, then took a sip of the coffee. "Mmm . . . is there caramel in this?"

"Yep, I thought you'd like it," he said as they made their way to Amanda's kitchen table. "What is it that I needed to help with? So we have our stories straight if she mentions it in the future." They sat down at the table.

Her eyes shifted up to the right as she contemplated. "How about you were thinking about adopting a dog and needed me to help with the decision?"

"But where's the dog? I wouldn't just look at a dog. I'd take him home."

"Why does it have to be a male?"

"You have something against male dogs? I feel offended."

"They pee everywhere," Amanda said. She grabbed the bag of doughnuts and shuffled through it until she found the chocolate covered with rainbow sprinkles. "They want to claim everything around them as theirs. Lift the leg and pssss . . ."

He laughed, then admitted, "You're not wrong, but I'm an excellent dog trainer. I would be able to nip it in the bud in just a matter of days."

"But what if it's a puppy?" she asked before biting into her pastry.

"A few weeks, tops," Dex said proudly.

"This I have to see," she challenged him.

"Now you're making me want to get a real dog to prove my abilities."

"Why don't you?"

"I'm gone most of the time during the week. It wouldn't be fair to the pup. But, you're usually home unless you're making deliveries or meeting up with clients. Why don't you get one?"

"I was thinking about it once upon a time. I don't know. Maybe I will," she said. Images of a lab-mix puppy sitting with her on her sofa popped into her head. She smiled.

"We should go to the shelter and check out some pups after we eat," Dex suggested with a smile.

"Maybe," Amanda said.

"There is no maybe. It's either a yes or a no."

"Who are you? Yoda?"

Dex laughed. "What's on your to-do list on this gorgeous Saturday?"

"I have to check if the DW hotel has an opening for the wedding. If they don't, I can check with parks and rec to see if I can reserve a spot either on the beach or at the park."

"A Christmas wedding on the beach," Dex reflected. "Only in SoCal."

"Want to come with me?" Amanda asked.

"Sure. Don't Rachel and Will need to go?"

"No, they said they're happy with any options and just reserve and let them know as soon as possible. I need to finalize it today to get started on the invitations and mail them out."

Three hours later, they left the DW Embassy Suites. Amanda had Rachel and Will on speaker from her cell phone. "You're in luck. The hotel had a cancellation last night. The reception hall is reserved for Christmas Day at two o'clock. The church has already been reserved for the ceremony. You were right; your mom made a sizeable donation to ensure it."

"That's great news. Thank you," Rachel said. They chatted for a bit longer as Amanda and Dex continued to walk toward Dex's car.

Dex unlocked the car and opened the door for Amanda. He sat in the driver's seat, turned the ignition, rolled down the windows, and patiently waited until Amanda was off the phone. After she tossed her cell phone into her purse, Dex asked, "To the shelter we go?" Dex waggled his eyebrows.

Amanda sat thoughtfully for a beat, then grinned. "Yes."

Fifteen minutes later, they walked from kennel to kennel. "I want to take them all home," Amanda said.

"Whatever you do, don't get a Chihuahua," Dex warned.

Amanda snorted and then asked incredulously, "What? Why?"

"They're evil." Dex pointed his right index finger at her. "See? See my finger?

You see that scar?" They stopped in the middle of the corridor between the kennels, and she reached out to touch his hand. She felt the same intense fluttering feeling in her stomach she'd experienced at the engagement dinner. Dex stiffened, but Amanda shook it off as uncertainty about committing to a dog. She lifted his hand closer to her and inspected it. She'd never noticed the scar before, but he had a half-moon indentation between his index knuckles. "I was twelve and had to get stitches. My grandmother's Chihuahua wanted me for lunch."

Amanda raised her eyebrows in surprise.

"I had pit bulls, German shepherds, Dobermans, labs, huskies, you name it. They were goofy, loving dogs. But Chihuahuas, they're the ones that should be on the bully-breed watch list."

"I never noticed that scar before," Amanda said.

"Promise me," Dex nearly begged. "No Chihuahuas."

"Yes, sir."

A woman with curly red hair and green eyes approached them and said, "Amanda, is that you?"

Amanda squinted her eyes, tilted her head, then straightened when she recognized the woman as a friend from high school. "Jasmine Watkins! What are you doing here? I thought you moved to New York!" Amanda shouted excitedly as she rushed to her. They embraced in a hug.

"I did, but I missed Beach City too much. So, I'm back to stay. I volunteer here when I can."

Dex cleared his throat.

"Oh, I'm sorry. Jazz, this is my neighbor, Dex. Dex, this is Jasmine, but I'm allowed to call her Jazz," Amanda said, placing her right hand over her heart. "If she likes you, she'll give you permission to call her by her nickname."

"Do you like jazz music or something?" Dex asked.

"Yep. I played the saxophone in the marching band back in the day. I was also in the jazz club. One of four members." She laughed. "The four of us decided to be a band recently. We play a little bit of everything. But enough about me, let's focus on the dogs. So, which one of you is looking for a dog to adopt?" Jazz asked, looking between Amanda and Dex.

Dex pointed a finger at Amanda. "She's adopting, but I'll be dog-sitting or borrowing her dog when I can."

"Are you looking for a particular breed, size, temperament?" Jazz asked.

"I'm open. I've been thinking about it for a while, but I'm just looking right now. To give me an idea and—"

"Not a Chihuahua or anything that yaps all day long. Or howls. No howling in the middle of the night. And she doesn't want one that's an escape artist and wants to poop on the neighbor's lawn. And she doesn't want one that crawls under fences or digs," Dex interjected.

"You know a thing or two about dogs, huh?" Jazz asked.

Dex nodded. "I've had a dog all my life. I just haven't had one for the past couple of years since I moved to Beach City."

"Well, he thought of things I didn't think of. But, he's right," Amanda said.

"Are you looking for a specific age?" Jazz asked.

"Not really. I'm open."

"Well, I have a few that come into mind. One is a senior lab. She just needs a good home. She pretty much chills all day and snuggles. We also have a mixed terrier named Hex. His owner passed away. The person who dropped him off said the owner found him on Halloween. We aren't sure what he's mixed with. He's guessed to be about three years old. Playful but likes to snuggle and loves blankets. He'll even wear sweaters and T-shirts. There's also a

German shepherd–lab mix. She's about two years old. She's watchful and notices everything, but she's also goofy."

Amanda grinned. "I'd love to see them all."

"Just remember, you can only get one," Dex warned.

Amanda pouted. "Right."

Two hours later, Amanda filled out an adoption application form for the mixed terrier, Hex. He was gray with white paws and a natural mohawk from his head down his back. Hex was scraggly and full of energy. After she filled out the paperwork, she handed it to Jazz. Jazz admitted, "Normally, we require visiting the home before we sign off on the adoption, but I know you and know Hex will be in a good home. You're free to take him now, or we can hold him here until you're ready to bring him home."

Dex jumped up and down. "We got a dog! We got a dog!"

"We?" Amanda laughed.

"Oh, come on, admit it. We see each other all the time."

"A crate, dog dish, toy, food, and water dish are included with the adoption fee. We'll give you enough dog food to last about a week."

“Let’s take him now,” Dex suggested excitedly. “We can stop at the pet store and pick out a leash and get him a few T-shirts.” His eyes were full of excitement.

Amanda laughed. “Okay, sounds like a plan.”

Chapter Five

On Friday night Amanda's doorbell rang. Hex barked excitedly and followed her to the door. Amanda opened it to find her niece, Lexi, standing there with her duffel and sleeping bag. For a moment, Amanda stared at her, then she remembered. "Oh, I forgot!"

Lexi dramatically placed a hand over her heart. "How could you forget about me?" She didn't wait for Amanda to respond. Lexi's attention immediately shifted to Hex. She dropped to her knees, still on the front porch, and squealed. "You got a dog!!! Eeee!!!"

Hex wagged his tail and appeared just as excited as Lexi. He put his paws on her bent knee and licked her face repeatedly. Lexi giggled.

"Well, that's one less thing to worry about. I wasn't sure how he'd react to people visiting."

"I love him!" Lexi shouted. "What's his name?"

"Hex," Amanda said. "Why don't we go inside before something crazy happens?"

Lexi and Hex moved into the house, and Amanda closed the door.

"Dad said you'll probably need help with some of the wedding planning stuff. I brought my craft kit just in case."

"We probably won't be working on any of the wedding stuff. I have two other kids coming over tonight."

"But you forgot about me?" Lexi asked, pouting.

"Yes and no. I forgot I'm watching kids tonight. You just reminded me."

"You need to write it down in a planner like you do for all your wedding clients. You need it for your personal life."

Amanda pointed a finger at her and admitted, "You're right." Changing the subject, she said, "I like your hair. Did it take long?" Lexi had her waist-length, light-brown hair in tiny braids.

"Thanks. Mom took me to one of her friend's houses in LA. It took all day, but it was fun. Except for when my head hurt from her pulling so hard," Lexi said as she made her way to the couch. She sat down, and Hex jumped on her lap. "So, who else is coming over?"

"The twins from down the street, Cari and Sheri."

Lexi grinned. "Oh yeah, they're fun. I wish we went to the same school."

"They'll be here in about an hour," Amanda said. "Are you ready for Halloween tomorrow?"

Lexi snorted and then said, "I was ready two weeks ago. I wanted to go to Knott's Scary Farm with a few friends, but Mom and Dad won't let me."

"You'd pee in your pants. It wouldn't be a good look for you."

"Just because that happened to you doesn't mean it will happen to me," Lexi chastised.

Amanda gasped. "Who told you that?" She grimaced from the memory from over ten years ago. Thankfully, she had brought a pair of sweatpants to change into, thinking it would get colder later in the evening.

"Dad, of course."

"I had coffee before we left for the park and then chugged a thirty-two-ounce Slurpee."

"Who drinks a Slurpee after coffee?" Lexi asked with a disgusted look on her face.

Amanda raised her hand in the air and then explained. "The guy was in a mask and dragging this can thing all around the park, scaring other guests. It was making all kinds of obnoxious scraping, creepy noises. He was groaning too. It got quiet for a bit, then the next thing I knew, I felt a hand on my shoulder. I turned, and there he was. You would pee too," Amanda declared.

Lexi crossed her arms. "I wouldn't drink all those fluids, and I hate coffee."

"I needed the caffeine to keep me awake and alert. But listen to me—you'd have nightmares," Amanda argued.

Just then, there was another knock on her door. Once again, Hex barked excitedly and followed Amanda to the door. Lexi also followed. Cari and Sheri stood with their duffels and sleeping bags. Their long, blonde, wavy hair was each pulled back in a ponytail braid. Their blue eyes widened. "You got a dog!" they shouted in unison. Lexi gestured for the girls to enter the house. She waved to her neighbors as they backed out of the driveway.

She was proud of how well Hex got along with the preteens. They all played well together. Around seven thirty, the doorbell rang. She was pleasantly surprised to find Dex holding two pizza boxes and a small chocolate cake on top. "I figured you required pizza and cake since I saw a few always-hungry monsters being dropped off," Dex said with a laugh.

"Hey, we aren't monsters. We're divas in training," Lexi countered.

"Monsters? We're models," one of the twins said.

"Who wants pizza?" Dex asked as he wandered into Amanda's kitchen. The girls followed him. Hex was at Dex's feet as he walked.

As they were eating, Amanda asked, "Would you girls like to help me with the wedding invitations next weekend? I'll pay with fresh-baked cookies."

The three young ladies agreed.

"Hey, Dex, I just thought of something," Lexi said.

"What's that?" Dex asked just before taking a bite of pizza.

"Would I have to call you Uncle Dex when you and Auntie finally admit you're in love and get married?"

Amanda choked and heaved. One of the twins rushed up behind her and started pounding on her back.

Dex stood frozen, but then spat out his pizza. He blinked, then realized Amanda was having trouble breathing. He quickly sprang to his feet, forced her out of her seat, stood behind her, and performed the Heimlich maneuver. A chunk of pizza flew out of her mouth.

She coughed. Her face was flushed.

Lexi handed her a glass of soda.

Amanda's eyes were watering.

"Are you okay?" Dex asked.

Amanda nodded as she took a sip of the bubbly fluid. She took a slow breath in and then out. "I'm good now. Thanks."

"So, answer Lexi's question," Cari urged.

Dex cleared his throat. "First, Manz and I aren't dating. We're friends. To be clear, she's my best friend. So no, you don't have to call me Uncle."

"Come on. You two are always together. Whenever I come over, you're here. Whenever Auntie comes to my house, most of the time, you're there too."

"So, what movie do you girls want to watch?" Amanda nearly shouted the question in desperation to change the subject.

"Grown-ups don't make any sense," Lexi whispered before taking a sip of her soda.

"You know, I've been thinking of adopting the senior lab," Dex said.

"Seriously?" Lexi asked. "See? You two are even dog shopping together."

"Totally in love and clueless," Sheri said.

"But Dex, you said you wouldn't be home enough." Amanda ignored the girls.

"I figured I could take him along with me on rides, and if you're okay with it, he could stay here with you when I'm gone for long periods," Dex said with pleading eyes.

Amanda felt her heart quicken a bit. "If you're sure he won't have accidents in my house, that's fine."

Dex grinned. "She's a female, remember? Her name is Shanook, but I'll call her Nook. Thanks."

Chapter Six

A week later, the girls were back at Amanda's house to help with the wedding invitations. She'd already cut out the paper doves, bells, and church steeples. She'd also printed out the written inserts. All that remained was the tedious task of pasting the cutouts onto the front of the invitation and writing out the addresses. Amanda took pride in her artistic ability to write in calligraphy. Lexi would be able to address half of the invitations since Amanda had taught her the rare skill.

"Cari, you're in charge of the doves. Sheri, you're in charge of the church steeples, and Lexi, you paste the bells. I'll stick on the ribbon. Once they're done, we'll wait for them to dry and then start stuffing the envelopes."

"Will *Uncle* Dex be coming over?" Lexi asked.

The twins giggled.

"Knock it off with that, Lexi," Amanda said, nearly pleading. She tried to ignore the fluttering of her heart. What was going on with her body lately whenever she thought of Dex?

"Dad said you have a crush on Uncle Will. But I told him you wouldn't be planning his wedding if you still did. Plus, I see how you are with Dex, and it's totally different. You look at Dex as if he's a part of who you are but you look at Will as if he's your brother. When you're with Dex, you lean into him and rest your head on him a lot, but with Will, it's like you avoid him, and you look like you're going to be sick when you stand next to him."

"That's because she still has a crush on Will. She gets nervous and doesn't know what to say to him," Sheri explained. "Cari gets that way when Tim just says hi to her. She can't even say hi back. She turns red and runs away."

"But she's more comfortable with Dex," Lexi argued.

"Stop talking about Tim and me." Cari nudged her sister. "But I agree with Lexi. Amanda should marry Dex. They would have cute kids, and their marriage would last because they were best friends first."

"We aren't—" Amanda started but was cut off when Lexi raised her hand to stop her.

"You can deny it all you want, Auntie. But everyone knows you and Dex belong together."

Amanda fanned herself.

There was a knock on her door, and it was Dex.

Dex's heart skipped a beat when Amanda opened the front door. What was wrong with him? It was Manz, for crying out loud. She wasn't in a fancy evening gown or anything. She had her hair piled up on top of her head in a messy half-bun with frays of hair sticking out. She was wearing an oversized lavender T-shirt that hung a bit off her shoulders, exposing the straps of the black sports bra she was wearing, and gray cutoff sweatpants. She was barefoot, and her toes were painted a bright red. That strange stirring in the pit of his stomach intensified.

"I . . ." He couldn't remember why he'd knocked on her door. There was a valid reason, but he couldn't remember for the life of him.

"Want to help with the invitations?" she asked.

"Sure," he said, relieved she spoke before he made a fool of himself.

The twins and her niece were deep in conversation when he appeared at the table. "You can stuff the envelopes," Amanda directed.

"That's what I do. Seal the deals," Dex said.

Amanda met Rachel and William at the Palm Hills Mall the following day. They were standing between the food court and the kids' play area. "Thank you for meeting us," Rachel said.

"You're welcome," Amanda said wearily. "What's up?"

"We need to register, and neither of us knows what we're supposed to do."

"Oh, right," Amanda said. "I usually don't help with the registry. The bride and groom usually just do it themselves."

William shrugged his shoulders as if he was clueless and just doing what he was told.

"Right," Rachel whispered.

Not for the first time, Amanda wondered what was going on with Rachel. She had always appeared to be a super confident person in the past. But, ever since the wedding announcement, Amanda was starting to see Rachel's softer, more insecure side. She surprised herself by wishing that William wasn't there so they could talk.

Rachel wrung her hands and shifted side to side. "I'm sorry, Amanda. I know I keep asking you to do things you normally don't. I just don't know what I'm doing, and I'm not myself."

Amanda looked between William and Rachel. "What's going on?" she asked William directly. He wrapped his arm around Rachel and pulled her closer toward him protectively. Amanda could see pure love radiating between the two of them. She found herself smiling. Amanda was happy for him. She realized for the first time she wanted him to be happy, and if Rachel made him happy, Amanda would be happy for them. But she realized that both Rachel and William appeared solemn.

"What's wrong?" Amanda asked. "Tell me."

Rachel looked up at William; he nodded, then she said in a whisper, "I'm pregnant."

"Okay," Amanda said. She wasn't surprised. She knew there had to be a reason why they rushed to get married.

"You're not surprised?" Rachel asked.

"Um, no," Amanda said.

"I'm not thinking clearly, and like I've said a million times. I don't know what I'm doing."

"Amanda, we both know you're busy, but neither of us knows what we're doing. We're under a lot of pressure with our work lives, then the wedding, the baby, Rachel's mother." William paused to take a deep inhale, then exhaled exasperatedly. "If it were up to us, we'd have gone to city hall or Vegas. But her mother, being who she is . . . it just gets overwhelming."

Rachel nodded.

"Okay," Amanda said with understanding, then gestured for them to follow her. She walked with them to one of the bigger department stores. "We'll go to guest services, and they'll help you sign up for both the wedding and baby registries. You can go to the baby store and register there too. I think you should consider registering at a bargain store too. Not all of your guests will be able to afford much at the bigger, ritzier store." Amanda was thinking from her perspective.

"My mother will flip when she sees we're on the baby registry," Rachel said.

Amanda held her hands up in surrender. "It's completely up to you. There have been plenty of brides and grooms who have registered for both. These are modern times. It's not a huge scandal to be pregnant before your wedding."

"We'll think about it," William said.

"Once guest services gives you the scanning guns, I'll leave you two alone."

"Thank you," Rachel and William said in unison.

Chapter Seven

On Wednesday morning, Amanda sifted through the mail on her coffee table while Hex slept next to her on the couch. His head was resting on her lap. She'd tossed yesterday's mail there without looking at it in a rush to run to her bathroom. Now, she saw the bills.

She'd received a late notice from the DMV. Her registration tags were overdue by a few weeks. "Oh crap!" It was one of the bills she kept putting aside, thinking she'd do food deliveries at some point and pay it off instead of charging it. Now, she owed more than what she did before.

"Ugh!" She glanced at the time on her phone. It was nearly eight. The breakfast rush would soon start. She glanced at her planner and saw that she had no wedding or other parties to work on today, so now would be a good time to log on to the food-delivery app. It was possible she could make enough money in the next few hours to pay her registration. If she had extra hands, it would happen. Often, she'd get a new order while she was driving and wouldn't be able to accept the order. But if someone else were in the car with her, she'd be able to get more orders.

Her niece was at school, so she was out of the question. She could ask Dex, but she was feeling guilty. She didn't want to be that neighbor who constantly needed help. She'd have to suck it up and do the deliveries independently. It might take her all day to get the money she needed, but she'd get it done. "Want to go with me, Hex?" He lifted his head and looked up at her. She thought about it for a bit. "That might be a bad idea. I'll be hopping in and out of the car a lot, and it might not go so well if someone saw you next to their food." Hex tilted his head from side to side. "I'll bring us back some fries when I'm done. How's that?" He wagged his tail.

Amanda was in denim shorts, a white tank top, and tennis shoes twenty minutes later. Her hair was slicked back and draped over her right shoulder in a single braid. She locked her front door and headed to her silver Toyota Corolla. She'd clicked her key chain to unlock her car when she saw Dex watering the plants hanging from his front porch. "Hey, Dex," she said with a wave.

He looked up and stopped what he was doing, then headed her way.

She groaned. She didn't have time to talk. She had money to make. She got into her car, started it, then rolled down the windows. She hoped he would get the message she had things to do.

"What are you up to?" Dex asked after he leaned into the passenger-side car window.

"I'm about to make food deliveries. I found a bill I forgot about."

Dex frowned. He didn't like the thought of her out there alone, jumping in and out of her car and delivering food to random people all around Beach City. "Mind if I tag along?" he asked. "I can click the accept or decline button while you're driving. That way, you'd be able to get more orders and done sooner."

She smiled. "Yes, please. Only if you're sure. I don't want to be that needy neighbor."

"Of course, I'm sure, and give me a break. You've always been that needy neighbor," he said with a laugh.

"Ha! Not funny." Amanda pouted.

"Give me a sec. I need to lock up and grab my keys."

"Okay," Amanda said. While she waited, she logged on to the food-delivery app and clicked on the button that indicated she was available to accept orders. Just as Dex was getting into the car, her phone dinged, announcing an order was ready for pickup. She clicked the accept button and then handed her phone over to Dex. He buckled up, and off they went.

She was fortunate to receive a few back-to-back orders. A couple of hours later, she had already earned half of what she needed to pay for her registration. "Since it appears to have slowed down a bit, how about we take a break, and I treat you to a coffee and a bite to eat?" Dex said.

"Ooo, sounds good," Amanda said. "I promised Hex I'd bring back some fries when I'm done."

"Okay, I'll remind you later," Dex promised. "And it will be my treat too."

"You don't have to treat me all the time," Amanda said. "I'm not a charity case, you know?"

"Which is exactly why I'm treating you. You do too much. I like to see you relax every once in a while," Dex said.

"You do a lot too. You're always on the go and taking care of other people. Maybe I want to treat you sometimes," Amanda said as she drove to a nearby coffee shop. "So what happened? I thought you were going to adopt the senior lab?"

"Someone beat me to it," Dex said.

"Well, I'm glad she found a home."

They placed their orders a few minutes later and waited at a small round table when

Dex changed the subject and said, "I've wanted to ask you but keep forgetting. What's with you and that woman Caroline?"

Amanda grumbled, then explained, "She bullied me throughout junior high and high school. She's the reason I won't let anyone call me Mandy."

"Oh," he said.

"Remember how I told you I was once overweight?"

He nodded.

"She tormented me with the chant 'Mandy likes candy.' She'd throw candy at me and just make me feel awful. So many times I had to run to the bathroom and lock myself in a stall and cry my eyes out."

"Is that one of the reasons you don't like Rachel?" he asked.

"It was, but now that I'm getting to know her, I honestly don't understand why she and Caroline are friends. When she first came to my English class in the seventh grade, she looked at me and smiled. I thought she would sit next to me, and I had this little vision that she would be my new best friend."

"What happened?"

"Caroline called her name and told her to sit next to her. Caroline had been assigned to welcome Rachel at the beginning of the day, and they became besties after that."

"Oh," Dex said, feeling a little sad for the younger version of Amanda. Dex's name was called, alerting them their order was ready. He gestured for Amanda to stay seated while he grabbed the coffee and bag of pastries. When he returned, he handed Amanda her cup and coffee cake.

She inhaled the scent of hot mocha and smiled. "Mmmm. I can't wait for it to cool off and take a sip." She took a bite out of the cake and bounced happily in her seat.

"You're easy to please," Dex complimented with a grin.

"I've limited my sugar and carb intake ever since my junior year in high school. So it's always a treat when I finally have it."

He switched the subject back to Caroline. "So it must be tough for you to work on this wedding, not just because of Will but also because of Caroline."

She soured and stiffened a bit in her seat. Dex thought perhaps it was a mistake to have broached the subject. But to his surprise, she said, "You know, I thought it would be difficult, but after the initial shock and hurt. I'm okay now. I've grown and changed a lot since high school. I don't respect Caroline, so she doesn't have permission to hurt me. She's just annoying. As for William . . ." She sighed, then said, "I realized the other day that I just want him to be happy. I know nothing could or would happen between us. It was a ridiculous crush and nothing more. I mean"—she paused, cleared her throat, then continued—"it was a real thing, but my feelings for him were more like hero worship. I put these unrealistic lenses on when it came to Will. I always envisioned him rescuing me at some point in my life and having a fling with him, but I never really saw him as someone I would marry or anything."

"Do you think you'd ever want to get married?" Dex surprised himself by asking the question.

"Yes and no. I want to have a family of my own, and kids, but the husband part? I don't know if anyone would want to live with me for life. He'd get bored with me."

"I want to spend the rest of my life with you," Dex blurted. He blinked, shifted uncomfortably in his seat, then coughed. "I mean"—he cleared his throat, then continued—"I can't imagine not seeing you every day. Even if it's just a wave."

Amanda flushed, surprised by his admission. Her eyes watered a bit, then she smiled again. "Thanks, Dex. I feel the same way. But we're neighbors. We don't live together. There's a difference."

"Maybe, but just to be clear, stop doubting yourself. You're a catch, Manz.

There are plenty of men who would bend over backward to see you smile."

Amanda finally took a sip of her coffee. It was the perfect temperature. She chugged, clapped her hands, then said, "We've gotta get back to work. I don't want to be doing deliveries all night." She stood up.

He gulped down his coffee too, then followed her out to the lot.

They continued with the deliveries for a couple more hours, and then each of them yawned. "One more order," Amanda said. "I've exceeded my goal thanks to you, but I'd like a few more dollars for cushion."

"Okay," Dex said just as the order was received. "Hey"—he glanced at the phone—"it's from the steak house, and it's a big order. You should get a good tip for this one."

Amanda grinned. "Let's go." She drove to the steak house, picked up the order, and got back into the car to find Dex frowning as he looked at the phone.

"What?" she asked wearily.

"You're not going to like this," Dex said.

"What? Tell me. Where's the order going?"

"Caroline," Dex mumbled. He turned the phone so that she could see. There was a photo of Caroline and her address.

"Great. Just great."

"I could take it to her if you'd like," Dex offered.

"No." Amanda shook her head as she buckled her seat belt. "I can handle it. She probably already received a notification with my photo to let her know I'm delivering it to her."

"Are you sure?" he asked.

"Yep," she said, lifting her chin.

A few minutes later, Amanda parked in front of Caroline's two-story house. Dex passed her the order, and she took a deep breath before getting out of the car and making the journey to the front door. As predicted, Caroline opened the door with a snarky expression on her face. Her blue eyes were uninviting. "Mandy Candy, I thought you were a successful wedding planner to the stars."

"Event planner," Amanda corrected, handing over her food. "I never said I planned for celebrities."

"It must be hard for you to deliver food. Don't you worry you'll gain all that weight back?"

"Not at all. I'm comfortable and confident enough with who I am. I'm in control of what I allow in my body. I'm also in control over how I handle others' thoughts and opinions."

Caroline tilted her head.

"Caroline, I don't know why you always had this need to target and bully me, but you aren't important to me. Your opinion and words don't mean anything to me. Perhaps one day, you'll grow up and realize you may be beautiful on the outside, but you're ugly on the inside. I pray for you to change your ways. It's not a good look for the soul. Good night," Amanda said calmly, turned, and walked away.

"Hey, was that Amanda?" she heard someone, a man, ask. The voice sounded so much like William. She rushed to the car before anyone could stop her.

Chapter Eight

On the second Friday of November, Dex looked out his living room window and thought about Amanda. He admired her. She was able to face her teen bully and her old crush. Well, she ran away from her crush, but she handled herself well. He hoped he'd never have to face his ex-wife or the man who threatened his life with a simple look. He thought he'd closed off his heart, but Amanda was opening it a little bit every day. She managed to make him smile every time they hung out. He felt protective of her. He wanted to see her all the time. Like, right now. He was trying to think of a reason to ring her doorbell. He glanced down at his watch. It was almost six. He sent her a text.

I'll be over in about forty minutes with dinner.

He stared at his phone for a little over a minute. Amanda replied with a simple thumbs-up emoji. He grinned.

He called their favorite Chinese restaurant and ordered for pickup. Before grabbing the order, he stopped at the grocery store and bought a cheesecake and a bottle of sauvignon blanc.

He felt butterflies in his stomach as he knocked on her door. "Well, that's new," he whispered to himself. "Get a grip."

Amanda opened the door wearing denim cutoffs and a formfitting peach V-neck T-shirt. Peach was now his favorite color. She had her curls down today. She was beautiful. "Hey, Manz." He felt his heart race a bit.

"Hey, Dex." She flashed him her perfect smile. "What's up with this?" She gestured to him from his head to his feet and back up again. He realized she noticed he dressed up a bit. He was in khaki dress slacks and a pressed white button-up shirt, and he was clean shaven. Hex was next to her, looking up at him and sniffing the bags of food.

He cleared his throat and then said, "I thought how proud I am of you. You faced your childhood bully and your crush. I decided I'd treat you to some of our favorites. You deserve it."

"Oooo . . ." She took the bag that held the cheesecake and wine from him and carried it into the kitchen.

He followed her and placed the containers on the table. "We've got vegetable fried rice, kung pao chicken, orange chicken, chow mein, and egg rolls."

She smacked her full lips. "Thanks, Dex. This is great."

He felt his stomach flutter again. *Flutter?* he asked himself. *Since when does anything in me flutter? Good grief.*

She'd already set out the plates and utensils. She wandered over to one of her upper cabinets and pulled out two wineglasses. Dex watched her for a moment, appreciating her curves and rear end. He'd never noticed her figure. Why was that? She was his best friend but . . . She turned, and he blinked to help himself redirect his attention to the task at hand. Dex opened the wine and poured them each a glass. They dished up their food and then sat down.

"So, how are the wedding plans going?" Dex asked. "Do you need help with anything?"

"Not yet. The guys go for their tuxedo fitting next weekend. I'm meeting with the band tomorrow to give them the down payment. I'm proud to say that it's going smoothly," she said before taking a bite of orange chicken.

"Uh-oh," Dex said.

"What?" Amanda asked, concern filling her voice.

"Didn't you just jinx the whole wedding?"

Amanda rolled her eyes. "No, it's fine. It's going to be great. I visualize the whole thing. It's fine."

Dex tilted his head.

"Really," she said. "It's fine."

"Okay," Dex said before taking a sip of wine.

They continued discussing the wedding as they ate, then shifted to movies, sports, and books. "Hey, what are you doing for Thanksgiving? Want to do what we did last year?" Amanda asked.

Last year, they went to her parents' house for a lunch feast and then to his sister's house for dinner. "Absolutely. I can't miss out on your mom's pecan pie."

She grinned. "And I can't miss out on your sister's pumpkin pie."

They clinked their glasses together.

After a few seconds of silence, Dex asked, "So how are you really doing with planning this wedding now?"

Amanda poured more wine into her glass, took a sip, and said, "I'm okay." Then she shrugged. "More than okay now. Like I said before, I realized it was only a crush. Sure, it seemed so much bigger than that a few months ago, but now that I've seen how

Will behaves around Rachel, I see I never stood a chance."

Dex frowned. "So if you had a chance, though, you'd take it?"

"Not necessarily. A month or so ago, absolutely. Now? I can't really see it. I hardly think about him anymore. When I do, it's all about the wedding."

"Is there someone who has captured your interest?" he asked hesitantly.

"I'm not sure. Maybe," she answered mysteriously. Her eyes glinted when she peered at Dex over the rim of her glass.

He wasn't sure if it was the wine, but the look she'd just given him caused a stir below his belt he hadn't felt in a long time. It was longing and desire.

"What about you?" she asked.

"What do you mean?"

"You never talk about your ex-wife or anyone you're dating."

He gulped wine and said, "I try not to think about it."

"Why? Is it that painful?"

"Not anymore. I just feel foolish. I don't ever want to go down that road again."

"Have you been dating since you moved here? I never see you bring a woman home." Her eyes widened, then she said hurriedly, "Not that I'm spying on you or anything. I just—"

"It's okay, Manz." He smiled. "I get what you're asking. I—" He sighed. "I don't know why, but I haven't been dating anyone. Sure, I hooked up with a few random women when I first moved here, but I don't know. It just isn't my style to have one-night stands."

"But you aren't ready for a real relationship yet either?"

"Right," he said.

"So what happened, if you don't mind my asking? You never told me why you got a divorce."

He looked to the ceiling briefly, figuring out how much to tell her. *This is Manz. I can tell her anything.* He found himself divulging everything, from the moment he met his ex to when his life was threatened.

"Wow!" Amanda exclaimed.

"Yep, wow," Dex said, pouring the rest of the bottle of wine into each of their glasses evenly.

"I'm so sorry you went through all of that," Amanda said. Her eyes were misty as if she were about to cry. "God. I wish I could take all your pain away." She sniffed.

"Are you about to cry?" he asked, surprised.

She sniffed again and sputtered, "Yep, I'm an emotional drunk . . . tipsy . . .

whatever I am." She hiccupped as tears started streaming down her face. "I can't st-st-stand seeing you hurt. To know someone hurt you like that and then to be threatened . . ."

He reached for her and hugged her. She moaned, and once again, he felt that stirring below his belt. "Uh boy," he said. "I better get home before I do something we both regret."

"No." She squeezed him tight. Her breasts were squashed against his chest. "I just want to hold you until all the bad memories leave you," she said.

"Um, Manz." He pried her arms from around him, then lifted her chin so that he could look into her eyes. "I'm a man who hasn't been with a woman in quite some time. Having you this close to me is triggering things that we may not want to trigger. I seriously don't want either of us to have any regrets."

She blinked, blushed, then said, "Oh. Oh . . . Okay."

"Good night," Dex said. Before he could talk himself into staying, he left.

Chapter Nine

William, Rachel, Matthew, and another man Amanda had never met before stood waiting for her the following Saturday afternoon in front of the tuxedo shop on Main Street. "You guys didn't have to wait for me out here. You could have just gone in," Amanda said.

"Rachel doesn't want to be confined in a small indoor space with us," Matt said.

Amanda laughed.

"Don't sound as if you're the victim here. I'm the one who has to play the role of Mommy whenever the three of you get together," Rachel said, exasperated.

"Pftt, please," William denied.

Rachel gave William a warning glare. "Would you like me to refresh your memories of when you watched the playoffs last year? The furniture that was unnecessarily broken?"

All three of them raised their hands in surrender. William said, "Okay, okay, you're right."

Matthew nudged the other man with his elbow, then said, "Peter, I'd like for you to meet my single sister, Amanda. Amanda, this is Peter. He's Rachel's single cousin."

Amanda turned on her professional smile and extended her hand. As they shook, she said, "I don't like being set up, which is obviously what my brother is trying to do. Despite that, it's nice to meet you. So you're the other groomsman?"

"Yep," Peter said with a grin, "and I'm with you on this sorry attempt to set us up. It's not gonna work."

Rachel stomped her foot while Matthew said, "Dang."

Amanda gestured toward the tuxedo shop. "Shall we go in? We have an appointment to keep."

Moments later, as the men tried on different jackets and in different colors, Amanda's mind drifted to Dex. *He'd look scrumptious in any of these,* she thought. An image of his dark-brown curly hair and matching dark-brown eyes popped into her head, along with his full, kissable lips. She wanted to kiss him a few times when they had dinner last week. It had nothing to do with the wine they'd shared. It had everything to do with him. She felt flutters in the pit of her stomach. Good flutters. Not nervous-and-want-to-throw-up flutters, but excitement-and-giddiness flutters. She couldn't wait to see him again. The realization didn't scare her either. She was beginning to feel bold and, honestly, impatient. She wanted Dex in the womanliest way possible.

"Be patient," she whispered. He'd only just told her the details surrounding his divorce. He wouldn't be rushing to get involved with anyone. He needed to progress on his terms. She knew it in her gut, but she also wanted to make him forget every horrible detail of his past relationship. "Ugh," she whispered. She leaned against a secured rollaway rack of sample coats.

"What's wrong?" Matthew asked as he stood beside her.

"Oh, nothing," Amanda denied.

"That groan and the expression on your face is not nothing. You wanna talk about it, little sis?"

"Nope, nothing to talk about," she said, crossing her arms.

"Does Dex have something to do with this nothing?" he asked suspiciously.

She took a step back as if she'd just been slapped. "What?" She was certain she was blushing. Amanda touched each of her cheeks.

Her brother grinned. "You heard me. By the red that just appeared on your face, I'd say I'm right in my assumption. You like Dex," Matthew said matter-of-factly.

"Of course, I like Dex. He's my neighbor."

"You like him more than as a neighbor and friend. You don't have to lie to me. Just tell him the way you feel. I think he likes you more than he's letting on too," Matt advised.

"I just don't want to mess up our friendship," Amanda admitted.

"I hear you, but just think of it this way—if I had never admitted my feelings to Kim, you might not have Lexi."

Amanda gasped from the thought. "Life without my mini-me?" She whispered the question.

"Think about that for a bit," Matthew said before rejoining the group.

Chapter Ten

Thanksgiving lunch at Amanda's parents' house was loud and full of family. Usually, her mother would insist on using the good China dining set, but there were too many family members; it was decorative recyclable paper plates and utensils instead. Dex sat next to Amanda with a plate full of food. "I thought you wanted pecan pie? How will you be able to eat it after all of that?" Amanda asked, gesturing with a fork at his overstuffed plate.

"Sounds like you're challenging me. Never tempt me when pie is involved. I accept the dare" Dex grinned just before shoving a forkful of food into his mouth.

They stayed at Amanda's parents' house for a few hours after eating to play games, then headed to Dex's sister's house for dinner. Dex rubbed his belly. "I love Thanksgiving. Did I ever tell you that?"

She laughed. "You told me that last year."

"I used to hate it. When I was little, my parents would drag my sister and me from house to house. It was always with stuffy clients of my dad's, so it was never fun. There weren't games to play. The food was bland. It wasn't seasoned the way your mom cooks. And your mom knows how to cook a turkey. Mouthwatering and just oooooh . . ." He continued to rub his belly. "And the pie . . . Do you know how to make the pie?"

"Yes, Dex. I know how to make the pie. I know how to make everything served at lunch today."

He grinned. "Thank God."

She laughed.

When they arrived at his sister's house, Dex said, "Now, you know it's the complete opposite of your family, right? It's just my sister, niece, and nephew. So it's quiet. We'll probably watch a Disney movie after we eat."

"Yes, Dex, I remember from last year, and I loved it. I'm a Disney dork, remember? Plus, I get your sister's pumpkin pie. I call it even."

They were surprised to find Dexter's sister, Monica, with a brand-new look. Her ordinarily long, dark-brown hair was chopped into a spiky pixie cut and bleached blonde. Her hazel eyes sparkled. They hugged and then immediately went down to the business of eating ham instead of turkey and more food. As Dex had predicted, they watched a Disney movie after eating dinner. He'd drifted off to sleep while Amanda enjoyed the movie and sang along with the kids and his sister. When the movie ended, the kids went off to one of their rooms to play video games. Monica gestured for Amanda to follow her into the kitchen as Dex continued to snore with his mouth wide open on the couch.

Monica and Amanda laughed. “He’s done this every holiday ever since he was little. Overeats then immediately falls asleep,” his sister said. “When he turned five, Mom and Dad threw him a birthday bash. When it was time for him to open the gifts, no one could find him. But, on a whim, I went into the laundry room and found him knocked out on a pile of clothes.”

Amanda giggled. “He must have been so cute.”

“If you call his butt in the air with his arms stretched out above his head cute, then okay,” Monica said with a chuckle. “Now look at him. Drool and snoring. Do you hear him from your house when he sleeps at night? The man is loud.”

“Yes, I do,” Amanda joked. When Monica’s eyes widened, Amanda added, “I’m kidding. No, I don’t.”

“So, Dex told me you’re planning the wedding for one of your old crushes.”

Amanda groaned. “Yep.”

“How’s that going?”

"It's going well. Hopefully… I mean... so far, so good."

"Do you still have a crush on the groom, or are you over him?" Monica asked.

"I've realized that I wasn't so much crushing on him as I was infatuated with the illusion I created of him."

"Ah-ha! Been there, done that. So what does that epiphany mean for you and my brother?" Monica asked with a raised, perfectly shaped eyebrow.

Amanda crossed her arms, shifted her eyes toward the ceiling, then asked, "Why is everyone trying to push the two of us into being more than friends?"

"Because you two belong together. You two are the only ones who don't see the obvious," Monica said as she crossed her arms.

Amanda took a small step backward. "I don't want to ruin our friendship. He's one of my best friends. Why would I want to do anything that could jeopardize what we already have?"

"What if what you already have can grow into something even more meaningful? I see the way the two of you are together. I see the chemistry. Obviously, I'm not the only one who sees it. I can even visualize the gorgeous kids you would make together. My brother deserves a family, and so do you. I think you two need to stop being afraid and take the leap."

Amanda bit her lip and was quiet as she contemplated Monica's words.

Footsteps approached, then Dex entered the kitchen, yawning and stretching. He rubbed his belly and said, "The food was delicious, sis. Thank you for the invite, as always." He yawned again. "Sorry for falling asleep. What were the two of you talking about?"

"Nothing!" Amanda exclaimed before Monica could say anything.

"Chicken," Monica challenged her.

Amanda's cheeks blushed.

Dex eyed each of them. "Ooooo," he said with a grin. "Sounds like a challenge. Did you know Manz never backs down from a challenge? Never dare her. Be warned. She'll never turn down a dare."

Monica grinned at her brother and then looked directly into Amanda's eyes with a glint. "I dare you. Leap."

"Still don't know what you're talking about," Dex said. He patted Amanda on the back. "But, listen to my sister. Don't tell her I said this, but she usually knows what she's talking about. Do what she says. Take the leap into whatever it is. What have you got to lose?"

You, she thought.

Chapter Eleven

On Friday morning, Amanda got out of bed crabbier than usual. She'd never been a morning person but what made it worse was that she didn't get much sleep. "Argh!!" she grumbled to no one. Amanda blamed it all on Monica and her challenge. She kept thinking about Dex. Not just Dex, but about Dex's body. That was new. She'd seen him without a shirt on a gazillion times and never gave it much thought. He tended to do yard work and wash his car without a shirt. She hadn't seen him without his shirt on for a few weeks. That that particular realization stuck out in her mind was something all on its own to note. But for whatever reason, thoughts of him shirtless kept popping up in her head. He had just the right amount of hair on his chest that made it so sexy. It wasn't so hairy that he looked like he belonged in a zoo, but just enough to cover his enormous heart. Just the right amount that she wanted to run her hands through it. She also wanted her hands to follow the happy trail that led down to his manly orgasm-producing part.

"Oh my God!" Amanda shouted as she pressed her palms to her eyes as if it would help eliminate the visions from popping into her head. "I need a shower." She fanned herself. "I need to get these thoughts out of my head."

Hex was at her feet. The puppy used his right paw to tap on one of her legs.

"Yes, sir. I will feed you your breakfast." But he rushed over to the back door instead of the kitchen. "Oh, right. Let's get you out first."

Fifteen minutes later, they were back inside. Amanda glanced at the calendar on her phone. "Right, cake tasting today at noon at Pineapple Coconut Bakery." She felt herself perk up a bit. Cake always perked her up. Of course, she'd have to go for a jog or bike ride later tonight, but it would be worth it.

Amanda arrived at the bakery on Main Street a few hours later. William, Rachel, and Matthew were already inside and sitting at one of the small round tables. Rachel beamed when Amanda walked in. William scooted a chair out for her. "Have a seat."

"Someone just went into the back to get the samples." Rachel said.

"Great," Amanda said. She sat down and then asked, "Where's Caroline? I thought she was joining us." She was relieved not to see her but wasn't holding her breath.

"Oh, she had another appointment, so she won't be coming," Rachel said.

Amanda let out a sigh of relief.

"My mom tried to invite herself, but thankfully she was called on set for a table reading for a new movie," Rachel said.

"Well, I think we have just the right number of taste testers. Too many, and it would take a while to agree on one flavor."

"Could we have more than one flavor?" William asked.

"Absolutely. With the number of guests you'll have, you can do two to three tiers. You could have a different cake for each level if you want."

"Yay," Rachel said happily.

Amanda tilted her head curiously at Rachel. She seemed to be getting more and more excited about the wedding. "It's nice to see you smile and be happy," Amanda said.

William smiled too. "It's cake. How could anyone be sad when they're about to eat cake?"

Everyone laughed.

A cart was wheeled out from the back of the shop by a man with dark-brown hair capped with a hairnet. He wore plastic gloves. "Hi, Amanda," the man said.

"Hey, Kevin, how are you?" Amanda greeted.

"Not bad." He parked the cart next to the table and then placed six different cake slices in front of them. Kevin also handed each of them a dessert fork and napkin. He gestured to each cake as he explained, "We have a slice of pineapple coconut, buttercream pecan, lemon, chocolate with raspberry, vanilla, and marble. We can change the filling to almost anything you'd like. We can also change the frosting."

"You guys can take a bite out of the pineapple coconut, but I call dibs on eating the rest of it," Rachel said. She'd already scooped up a forkful of vanilla and put it in her mouth. She was dancing in her seat.

"No carrot cake today?" Amanda asked, disappointed.

"Sorry, no," Kevin said. "We sold the last carrot cake for the day about an hour ago. I haven't had a chance to bake another one yet."

"Ah, man," Matthew whined.

"My mom doesn't want chocolate, carrot, or pineapple coconut," Rachel said.

"It's not her wedding," William said, aggravated.

"You're correct, but we both know how my mom is."

"We'll gladly provide you with your first-anniversary cake free of charge in any flavor you wish."

"So we don't have to freeze the top tier?" Rachel asked.

"No, many couples don't bother with that tradition anymore," Amanda explained. "You totally can if you want to, but I've learned that it doesn't taste right, and more often than not, the cake is thrown out."

"I have no idea what you two are talking about," William said before biting into the chocolate raspberry. He closed his eyes and moaned.

"Neither do I," Matthew said.

"It's right up there with not seeing the bride before the wedding. You save the top tier of the wedding cake and freeze it. Then on the first anniversary, you defrost and eat it," Amanda explained.

"Yuck." Matthew scowled. "Glad it's not happening. I'd have to steal it the day of the wedding and eat it on your behalf."

"And that's why you're a Slytherin," Amanda said.

Rachel's eyes widened.

"Oh no, here we go," William said. "Brace yourself."

Rachel playfully patted Amanda's arm. "Get out! I said the same thing! I didn't know you were into Harry Potter."

Matt rolled his eyes. "She's a dork. Of course, she is. And how many times do I have to tell you? I'm not Slytherin. The hat would have told me and everyone else I belong in Ravenclaw."

William dramatically dropped his head to the table, only barely missing one of the cake slices.

"Oh, please," Amanda and Rachel said in unison.

"I belong in Hermione's house," Matt argued.

"Well, Ravenclaw isn't it, but you don't belong in Gryffindor either," Rachel said.

Amanda high-fived Rachel. They grinned.

Matthew scowled at both of them and then reached for the lemon and marble cake slices. He stood up and walked to a separate table.

"Hey, we need to sample those too," Rachel whined.

"No, you forfeited it when you ganged up on me." Matthew sulked.

William finally lifted his head and said, "It's okay. We've already decided on a three-tier. Two cakes will be lemon, and the other will be marble."

Rachel nodded.

"I thought you said your mom doesn't want chocolate," Amanda said.

"Yes, so she won't eat the marble. She can have the lemon. William and I love chocolate, so we can compromise with marble but a cream cheese frosting. The lemon cake will have the same frosting."

"So if you guys already knew what you wanted, why the cake tasting?" Amanda asked, confused.

Rachel smiled as she rubbed her belly. "Because it's too delicious not to pass up. Am I right?"

Amanda laughed. "You're right."

Chapter Twelve

On Saturday, Amanda woke to Hex licking her face enthusiastically. She groaned and then giggled as Hex's efforts became more exuberant. "Okay, okay, I'm up. Geesh." Hex barked. "You wanna go outside, huh?"

Amanda yawned, then stretched. She slipped on her fuzzy black memory-foam slippers that felt like she was walking on clouds. Hex followed her out to the backyard.

As she watched Hex sniff all over, searching for the perfect spot to relieve himself, she heard familiar whistling. "Dex, you're up early!" she shouted near the neighboring wooden fence.

"Hey, Manz, how'd the cake tasting go?" he asked, peeking through one of the gaps between the panels.

"It turned out we didn't need to do the whole cake-testing thing. They already knew what they wanted. Lemon and marble."

"Honestly, any cake from that bakery is amazing. They can't go wrong with whatever they choose."

"I agree. It's just that Rachel's mom is picky, and I'm kind of afraid of her."

"Bah. You could take her down easily," Dex joked.

"Ha," Amanda said sarcastically. "What are you doing today?" she asked, changing the subject.

"I have a few clients to show houses to and then hopefully submit an offer or two. What about you?"

"Just picking out wedding decorations with Rachel, then hanging out with Hex."

"Sounds like a nice day."

A few weeks ago, Amanda would have dreaded spending time with Rachel, but she realized Rachel was turning out to be fun to hang out with.

"Well, I just needed to water a few plants out here. I have to go meet up with a client now. I'll call you later. Maybe I'll pick up dinner, and we can eat together at your place?"

Amanda smiled. "Okay, talk to you later."

At around eleven that morning, Amanda met Rachel at a local party warehouse store. Rachel was in a baggy tank top and denim shorts. She was fanning herself. "Only in California would we be wearing shorts and tank tops in late November. Geez, it's hot."

"Don't you have a pool? You can go swimming after."

"That's a brilliant idea. I just might do that," Rachel said as they walked inside the store.

Amanda was hoping Rachel would extend an invite to her to join her for swimming. Maybe they could even have a barbeque. She could have invited Dex, her brother, and sister-in-law too. She shook her head as if to shake the random thoughts out of her head.

"So where's Caroline? I thought she was going to join us," Amanda asked.

"She made up some cockamamie story. I feel like she doesn't want anything to do with my wedding," Rachel said.

"But she was at the engagement party. She was talking about planning your bachelorette party and the bridal shower."

"It's all a ruse for her," Rachel said. "Her father and my mom have worked together for years in the film industry. They depend on each other and have forced Caroline and me to be friends even though we've never had anything in common."

"Really?" Amanda asked, astonished.

They stopped in front of one of the wedding aisles. There were rolls and rolls of multiple tulle colors on one side, then rows and rows of wedding-themed candies and candy holders on the other.

"Yes, really," Rachel said. "Do you realize that I wanted to sit next to you the first day I arrived at school? You were the one who helped me pick up my pens when I dropped them all in the office that morning. You were wearing baggy jeans and a magenta T-shirt, and you had the cutest daisy earrings. I wanted to hang out with you."

Amanda blinked in surprise, then admitted, "I thought we would be friends too. But Caroline insisted you hang out with her. Once she sank her claws into you, I knew you wouldn't want to have anything to do with me."

Rachel nodded sadly. "It was all because of my mom and her dad. I don't think Caroline has her own voice, truly. She does everything for her dad's approval. She's afraid she'll lose her trust fund and then have to join the workforce like the rest of us. I love working. I love feeling like I'm accomplishing something and helping people. My mom tried using my trust fund to manipulate me, but I haven't touched it."

"I never knew that," Amanda said.

"Anyway, let's pick out the decorations," Rachel said excitedly.

“Right,” Amanda said, focusing on the task at hand. “We don’t have to worry about tablecloths or napkins. The venue will provide all of that. They’ll also provide the centerpieces, but you could add a few personal-touch items to the table.”

“Candy—we need candy at each place setting,” Rachel said.

“Would you like someone to also pass out these little bottles of bubbles at the church?” Amanda asked, holding up tiny white bottles. “Then, as you guys are walking out, guests can blow bubbles at you. The photographer can capture some nice photos too.”

Rachel gasped. “That’s brilliant! I love bubbles. The kids there will love them too. My mom wanted me to exclude children from coming to the wedding.” Rachel scowled. “How can you not have children at a wedding! It’s about family and creating a new family. I love children. She was so upset with me for getting pregnant, but did you know I was happy? She was the one who instilled fear and dread inside me. She’s the one that made me so wound up from the start, but William and I talked. I’m not allowing her to control me or this wedding anymore.”

Amanda was once again astonished by Rachel. She was unloading a lot of emotional truths. "I had no idea."

"Yes, my mom's hobby is terrifying me and anyone else around her. But, no more."

"Well, good for you," Amanda said, genuinely proud of her.

"Oh, look! Little baskets. These are so cute!" Rachel squealed excitedly. "We need to get one for each guest, and oh, we'll get this roll of red tulle and cut it so these candies can go in, and—" Rachel talked superfast and grabbed items off the shelf as if she were the character Flash from the comics.

"Wait, wait, wait," Amanda interrupted, holding her hands up to stop her. "Let me get a shopping cart, and we can get precut tulle, so we don't have to spend a lot of time cutting. We can use silver ties, or we could use gold if you prefer. We can get the baskets or get these little sleighs instead since it is a Christmas wedding." Amanda lifted the miniature Santa sleighs.

Rachel gasped, clapped her hands, then jumped up and down. "I love it! Yes, the sleighs instead of the baskets. And oh! Look!" She pointed to a super large bag of red and green M&M'S. There were plain and also peanut. "We can fill them with the M&M'S!"

Amanda grinned. She was getting excited and happy for Rachel. It was nice to see her enthusiasm compared to her earlier depressive state.

Later that evening, Dex called to tell her he was running a bit later than he anticipated. "If the offers are accepted, I could have possibly sold four properties today. I probably should not have said that out loud."

"Wow! That's amazing. Congratulations!"

"Oh, no, don't congratulate me—that's like a curse. But, thank you. This is a record for me. The most offers I've put in in one day were two." He cleared his throat. "Now I just wait for the replies. It's going drive me crazy until I know."

Amanda laughed. "Well, how about I pick up dinner and meet you at your place for a change?" she offered.

"That sounds like a plan. I should be done in about an hour. My clients will be stopping by shortly to sign some documents, and then I'll need to send it all off to the other realtor."

"Okay, see you in an hour," Amanda said, before hanging up.

Chapter Thirteen

On the first Saturday of December, Amanda's mother invited her to go dress shopping for the wedding. "Come with me. It'll be my treat. I'll feed you and pay for whatever dress you decide to wear."

"Oh, I was planning to wear the usual rose-colored dress I wear for all of my clients' weddings," Amanda said.

"That's what I thought you'd say, which is exactly why I insist on taking you shopping. You need a special dress for this wedding. William is like your brother. You need to jazz yourself up a bit for this one. Plus, I hear there will be a few celebrities at the wedding. So, you need to present yourself amazingly for potential upscale clients. Besides, you need to be pampered by your mom sometimes. You've been Miss Independent since the moment you left the house. Let me do this for you. Sometimes a mother needs to feel needed."

Amanda groaned, but she knew her mother was right, which caused her to grumble a bit. "Fine," she said begrudgingly.

"Don't take that tone with me, young lady. You know I'm only trying to help you. Besides, you should be happy that your mom is feeding you and dressing you."

Amanda closed her eyes briefly, then said, "You're right. I should be and am thankful and happy. Just not sure I can handle the pressure of celebrities as potential clients. I don't know if I'm that good."

"Oh, nonsense. You're brilliant at planning any event. You enjoy what you do, which makes you all the better. Stop being your worst enemy and acknowledge your talents and skills. You should be proud of yourself. You turned something that was a hobby into a career. I'll pick you up in an hour."

"So, how's that hunky neighbor of yours?" Amanda's mom asked. They were sitting at the food court at the Palm Hills Mall, opting to eat first before starting their shopping adventure. Amanda knew she needed a good dose of caffeine to keep up with her mom when they shopped. Her mom should be a professional racewalker with how she zipped and zoomed from one store to another. While Amanda had stopped at the coffee stand, her mom had grabbed them each a burger and fries from another restaurant.

"Dex is doing fine," Amanda said. She gulped her iced mocha latte.

Her mother studied her. "Just fine, huh?"

"As far as I know, yes. Why?"

"Is something going on between the two of you?" her mom asked before snagging one of Amanda's fries even though she had her own basket.

"Hey! Why do you always steal my fries when you have your own?" Amanda whined.

"I like the way you season yours, and you're always so strategic on where and how you spread your ketchup." Her mom grinned. "And don't think you tricked me by changing the subject. I'm still waiting for an answer."

Amanda shrugged, stole one of her mom's fries as retribution, then asked, "Why is everyone asking me that?" Her mom smacked her hand, but she kept the fry anyway.

"Because there's something there between the two of you, and you need to make a move already. Dex is a good guy." Her mom placed a hand over her heart. "Oh, and the grandbabies the two of you would make . . . " Her eyes misted. She fanned herself. "I can just see it. You two will have three babies, and they'll adore me."

"Three!" Amanda rolled her eyes. "I can barely take care of myself and Hex. How would you expect me to take care of three little humans?"

"It's happening. Deal with it," her mom said dismissively with a wave of her hand. "My visions are never wrong."

"I don't want to ruin the friendship and bond we have. I've never been good with relationships. What if we get together, and then we break up? What would I do, Mom?"

"Stop worrying about the breakup when you haven't even professed your love for him yet. Why worry about it? Focus instead on telling him how you feel. The two of you are already in love with each other. What if he says it out loud? What if he tells you that he's in love with you too?"

"But . . . I can't hold a conversation that long," Amanda said in a panicked whisper.

"What are you talking about?" her mom asked in confusion.

Amanda picked up her burger and then put it back down. She took another sip of her coffee. Her right leg began to bounce up and down. "That's always been why my relationships never lasted more than a few weeks."

"What do you mean?"

Amanda fidgeted with a napkin. Her mom placed a hand on top of hers to stop her from squirming. "Talk to me," her mom said softly.

"I'm too quiet."

"Nonsense." Her mom rebuked her declaration.

"No, really, I am. That was one of the other reasons Caroline used to bully me too. I was too quiet. People would ask me questions, and I would just give them a straight answer and not elaborate."

"If you were too quiet, do you think you'd have clients? Do you think Dex would be hanging out with you as much as he already does?"

"But, it's different. We're just friends, so there isn't any pressure. If we start dating, there'll be expectations. What if I can't live up to his needs? What if we run out of things to talk about after we get together?"

Her mom waved another dismissive hand at her. "You're fishing for things to worry about. Stop worrying. Everything will be fine. You tell him how you feel, and then ask him what his expectations as his girlfriend would be. Heck, ask him what he'd expect from his future wife. You aren't proposing to him, but you can start the conversation. Trust me. You two belong together. Your mama knows." Her mom squeezed her hand. "Talk to him."

Amanda chewed on her bottom lip.

"Let's eat these burgers before they get cold," her mom said before taking a big bite out of her own.

Chapter Fourteen

The next morning, Amanda met William and Rachel at DW Embassy Suites, where they planned to have their reception. They were scheduled for an eleven a.m. walk-through with the hotel's event planner. Just past the hotel's main lobby to the right were enormous double doors that opened into the reception hall. The floors were burgundy carpet; six shimmering chandeliers were above. A dance floor was just below the stage. "This is nice," Rachel said with a smile.

William nodded in agreement.

"There'll be balloons strung into an arch on the stage. The wedding party can sit on the stage or just below. It's up to you."

"On the stage. It's our day," Rachel said confidently.

"Where will the band perform?" William asked.

"Oh, right," Rachel said thoughtfully. "Didn't think of that."

"They can set up over there to the right of the stage in the corner. The hotel provides speakers and amplifiers, but the band will be bringing their own equipment."

“And you confirmed they’re still available?” William asked.

“Yep, they’ll send me another confirmation email shortly,” Amanda said.

A woman with a navy-tailored suit and carrying an iPad entered the hall. “I apologize for being late. I was on an unexpected call.”

“Oh, no worries. We weren’t here that long. Rachel, William, this is Lexi Michaels. She’s the event organizer here at the hotel.”

“Nice to meet you.” She did a general wave at them. She took a deep breath and said, “The hall can hold up to six hundred people. We can open the wall right over there.”

“Oh, dear Lord, please do not tell that to my mother. We’re happy with one hundred, but most likely one fifty or two hundred will be coming,” Rachel said.

“We need a final count with the dinner plate preferences by next week. Chicken, beef, or veggie.” Lexi made a note on her iPad and then asked, “And I have it down that you decided on your bakery rather than ours, correct?”

“Yes, they’re going with Pineapple Coconut Bakery,” Amanda answered on their behalf.

“Oh, I love that place. Honestly, sometimes the cake here can be a bit dry, but you didn't hear that from me. We'll provide appetizers to all the guests within fifteen minutes at the start of the reception so that they can eat and settle down while you're taking wedding photos. Since this is a smaller party, the dance floor will be clear and ready to go for the first dance after dinner. We have a florist who can provide flowers for each of the tables, or you can hire your own. If you plan to hire your own, I hope you've already done so. It's getting too close to the wire, honestly."

"My mother already arranged it. She insisted on red and white roses for each table. A florist should be in touch with you soon," Rachel replied.

Lexi tapped more notes into her iPad. "Have all guests made room reservations?" she asked. "We have an entire floor reserved for your wedding. They're all booked, but if anyone hasn't made a reservation, I need to be notified, well . . . last week, honestly. It's Christmastime. We have only a few extra rooms available."

Rachel started to fan herself, and she turned a bit flush. "Uh boy," she said.

"Babe, are you okay?" William asked. Rachel wobbled a bit as if she was suddenly losing her balance. He quickly reached for her elbow and waist to steady her. Amanda rushed to her other side.

"Just felt a bit light-headed for a sec," Rachel said before taking a deep breath.

Lexi quickly dragged one of the cushioned chairs toward her. Amanda and William guided Rachel to sit.

She fanned herself a bit more. "I think I accidentally locked my knees there for a minute. I'm sorry."

"Which reminds me. I need to make sure I mention that to the wedding party. Don't lock your knees while standing during the ceremony," Amanda said.

"Right," William said.

"Why don't we all just take a seat here," Lexi offered, gesturing to the table near Rachel. "I apologize. I should have offered when I first arrived."

They continued discussing the plans for the reception for another hour. Amanda's cell phone dinged, announcing a new text message just as they were wrapping up. When Amanda finally glanced at the message, she said quietly, "No, no, noooo . . . this isn't happening."

"What? What's wrong?" Rachel asked.

"The band just said they accidentally double-booked. They aren't able to play for your reception."

"No!" William said. "I already paid them the down payment. They promised."

Rachel placed her head on the table.

"I'll fix this. I'll figure it out. It's what I do," Amanda said. She hoped she sounded and appeared confident, but she was sure she heard the doubt and shakiness in her voice.

"If all else fails, we have a system where someone can plug in their smartphone and play a playlist over the speakers. It won't be a complete loss," Lexi offered.

"My mother will not let us hear the end of it. We need a live band. Not just any band—an excellent band," Rachel said, muffled. Her head was still on the table.

"Are you sure you can fix this, Mandy?" William asked.

Amanda's back stiffened from hearing the nickname she hated the most, coming from the guy she once envisioned marrying, and cringed. She wanted to tell him never to call her that again, but she decided to be professional instead of personal. She forced herself to sit up straighter and said, "Yes. Leave it to me."

"I don't know what I'm going to do," Amanda said a few hours later. She was sitting on Dex's porch wearing denim shorts, a plain white T-shirt, and dark blue plastic flip-flops. Her hair was piled on top of her head in a messy, curly bun. "How in the world am I going to find a decent band in less than a couple of weeks before Christmas?"

"If all else fails, I can play music from my phone. I have plenty of good tunes that are suitable for a wedding."

"Celebrities will be there." Amanda groaned. "Rachel's mom only wants a live band."

"What do Rachel and Willy want? It's their wedding, not her mom's."

"They wanted to elope," Amanda said.

"I rest my case," Dex said proudly.

"But, if Rachel's mom is unhappy with this wedding, she'll talk, and it'll reflect badly on me and everything I've been working so hard for."

"Oh," Dex said, then patted her gently on the back. "Right. We better think of something good and quick then, kid."

Amanda wanted to pull her hair out. First, William called her Mandy, and now Dex called her *kid*. She stood up. "Can you not call me that?"

Dex was taken aback. "What?"

"I'm not a kid. I'm not Mandy. I'm a woman with needs and desires just like Rachel is. God, can anyone see that? Can anyone see me?"

Dex stood up and reached for Amanda's hands. "Whoa, hold on there, Manz!" He shouted to catch her attention and prevent her from saying anything further. Then more gently, he said, "Calm down. Come here." He pulled her into a hug, "I'm sorry for calling you *kid*. I didn't mean anything by it." She began to relax into his embrace. He whispered, "If anyone can see you're a woman, it's me."

She took a deep breath through her nose and inhaled his soapy pine scent. Amanda wanted to stay in his arms. She rested her head on his shoulder. He held her tighter. They both moaned from comfort.

"Hey," Dex said, "didn't your friend at the pet adoption place say she played in a band?"

Amanda suddenly shoved Dex away from her and then started to jump up and down. "That's right! Jazz has a band. Oh my gosh! Yes, I have to call her."

She fumbled to get her phone out of one of the front pockets of her shorts. "I've been talking to her about Hex. This could be huge for her." She pressed Jazz's contact-info button on her phone. Amanda was so busy and eager to talk to Jazz that she hadn't noticed the flush appearance of Dex. He was shifting from side to side, adjusting his shorts, attempting to hide their hug's effect on him.

Twenty minutes later, she was jumping up and down. “She’s in! She said the band said yes.” Dex grinned.

Chapter Fifteen

On Wednesday afternoon, Amanda had one foot propped up on her coffee table while sitting on her couch with Hex next to her. She had cotton balls between each of her toes and a bottle of cherry red nail polish in one hand. She had just finished painting the baby toe when there was a knock on her door. "Fudgsicles and popsicle sticks," Amanda murmured. "At least they're all painted, right, Hex?"

Hex jumped off the couch, just barely missing a few of her toes on the ground. Amanda gasped, quickly checked her paint job, then breathed a sigh of relief when she saw they were still pretty. She wiggled and wobbled her way to the door, balancing only on her heels. Amanda peered through the peephole and saw Dex. She fanned herself and then reached up on top of her head. She yanked off the scrunchie and let her curls tumble, then she draped her hair over one shoulder.

When she opened the door, Dex blinked as if he had briefly lost his train of thought. "What's up, Dex?"

"Um—" he stammered. "I . . . hold on." He glanced down at his feet, then noticed her toes. “Bubble toes,” he said with a grin, and looked into her eyes.

She scowled. “Excuse me?” Amanda attempted to put her hands on her hips to express her attitude, but it didn’t quite work because she momentarily lost her balance.

He caught her before she fell, then explained, “It was a compliment. You make me think of that Jack Johnson song, ‘Bubble Toes.’”

“Oh,” she said, leaning into him. “I like that song.” She smiled.

Dex was still holding her. His hands were around her waist. Their faces were close to each other. Just an inch or two more, and they could kiss. They were staring at each other’s lips. She cleared her throat. “So . . . you wanted to ask me something?”

“Oh.” He let go of her, and she leaned against the wall.

“Your brother called me. He invited me to the bachelor party,” Dex said. He was grinning again. His dimples were exposed, and his brown eyes were glimmering.

“Well, that was unexpected but cool of him. Don’t tell him I said that, though. I can’t let him know I thought any of his actions were cool.”

Dex chuckled. “I just want to make sure you were okay with me going.”

She tilted her head curiously at him. "You know you're a grown single man, right? Why would you need my permission for anything?"

His face flushed, then he said, "Well, you know, your brother has a wild reputation, and I just respect your opinion. I just don't want to do anything that could make you feel uncomfortable."

"Aww," Amanda said, "thanks for that, Dex. My brother once upon a time was wild-and-crazy but ever since he married my sister-in-law, he's a bit boring. You will most likely play poker and drink the whole night. Maybe one of the other guys will surprise you with a stripper or two."

Amanda wasn't sure, but she thought she saw a flicker of disappointment flash across Dex's face.

"Well," he clapped his hands once, then said, "guess I'll be going."

"Hey, do you want to go halves on a wedding gift? We can get them a better one if we do it together," Amanda asked.

"Do it together," he said slowly. Then he licked his lips and said, "Sounds like a good plan. I'm in."

This time Amanda flushed. She wasn't sure, but it felt like Dex was flirting with her in so many ways.

“I’ll see you later,” he said suddenly, and was gone.

Later that evening, there was another knock on her door. This time when she opened it, she found Rachel. She was sweaty and disheveled, unlike her typical, well-put-together self. Rachel was wearing mint green stretchy shorts and an oversized white tank top. “I’m sorry for showing up unannounced. I was visiting with my mother, and she just kept going on and on about all the things she hoped to see at the wedding. And she kept making so many of her subtle, cruel criticisms that I just left. I ran out the door and kept running.”

Amanda’s eyes widened. “You ran here? From your mom’s house? Doesn’t she live up that hill like, four miles away?”

“Three,” Rachel said, still gasping for breath. “It’s okay. I run five miles every weekend.”

“But you’re pregnant.”

“My doctor said it’s fine. He encouraged me to do all the physical activities that I used to do before becoming pregnant. But in the last trimester, I’ll have to slow down.”

"Oh, okay," Amanda said. She opened her door wider and then gestured for her to come inside. "I'll get you a glass of water."

"Thank you," she said. Hex came up to greet her. He licked her bare legs. "Oh, he's a cutie. Did you adopt a dog?" Rachel said with a little laugh.

Hex trotted behind them as they made their way into the kitchen. Amanda filled a glass with ice and water from the refrigerator dispenser. They both took a seat at the table. Hex sat next to Amanda, resting his head on her feet.

"I guess the whole cold-feet thing is real," Rachel said. "My nitpicking mother doesn't help the situation."

"Doesn't Caroline live just a few houses down from your mom?" Amanda asked.

Rachel frowned. "I suppose I could have gone to her house, but honestly, she can be just as critical or sometimes worse than my mother."

"Oh, I'm sorry," Amanda said.

Rachel waved her hand. "There's nothing for you to apologize for. I should apologize for intruding on you like this. I hired you to be my wedding planner, not my shrink. But Caroline hasn't exactly been there for this whole wedding or my pregnancy. It feels more like she's been avoiding me."

"Oh, wow. But, I thought you guys were just hanging out a couple of weeks ago?"

Rachel frowned again. "Why would you think that?" She gulped water.

"When I dropped off food at her place, you and Will were there, right?"

Rachel's face turned pale. "What? What do you mean?"

Amanda thought back to the day she delivered food and tried to recall if she had heard Rachel's voice. "Oh my gosh," she whispered.

"It all makes sense now," Rachel said as she paled. "I—"

"Rachel, are you okay? It could be completely innocent. You have to talk to them."

Rachel rose to her feet. She started to tremble.

"Sit down, please. You're in shock. I'll go get a blanket, and we can talk."

"No." Rachel held her hand up and shook her head. "I've troubled you enough. I need to go. But, you're right. I need to talk to them. But don't worry, I won't bother you anymore. The wedding is off." Amanda didn't get the chance to talk to her because Rachel rushed out of the house and took off in a run.

Less than an hour later, Amanda received many phone calls and text messages. Messages from her mother, her brother, Rachel's mom, William, Caroline, and one of the groomsmen. She thought of turning her phone off, waiting a few hours, and praying for everything to work out independently. But, to her shock, there was banging on her door that could not be ignored. It was Rachel's mother. "You will fix this. You broke it. We are paying you. You will fix this, or I will ruin you before you even get started. Do you understand me?"

She had never met Rachel's mom up close and personal. It was always from way, way afar at occasional school events, but she'd never been this near to her. Amanda opened her mouth to say something but no coherent words would come. Instead, she stammered, "I… um… I…" A superstar was standing on Amanda's front porch demanding she fix her daughter's love life or she'd personally destroy everything she'd worked so hard for. The dream she created with her grandmother. All because William couldn't keep it in his pants.

She felt strength begin to bubble up inside her due to the anger that was boiling to the surface. Amanda stood taller. "First, hello. Nice to meet you," Amanda said sarcastically. "Second, this isn't my fault—it's William's. Don't you dare stand on my grandmother's porch and accuse me and threaten me of anything! You want to use your star power to ruin a hardworking innocent person's life, by all means, go ahead. Little me won't be able to stop you. I don't have the power to fix this. This is between your daughter and William and has nothing to do with me."

"I heard you always had a crush on William. You deliberately did this so the two of them would break up, and then what? You get him all to yourself?"

"Give me a break, lady. You don't even know me. You don't know anyone other than yourself or someone who can advance your acting career. Why don't you stop criticizing people and get to know them? Have you thought about how hurt Rachel is right now? Or are you only concerned with how this will reflect on you?" Amanda held her hands up. "Those are rhetorical questions. I don't expect or want to know the answers. For your information, I had planned to call William and Rachel and get the two of them together to talk it out. I still plan to. But, just to be clear, it has nothing to do with you or your wicked threat. It has everything to do with your daughter, who I now consider a friend. Now, please leave, or I'll call the police."

Rachel's mom gasped, but then closed her mouth and turned to leave.

Chapter Sixteen

Amanda had tried calling Rachel and then William many times, but neither would answer her calls. She finally decided to grab her keys and drive over to William's house to see if he was there. Just as she pulled her front door open, William walked up her steps. "I don't know what to do. I don't know how to fix this," William said lowly.

"Why'd you do it? How could you cheat on her? And with Caroline of all people?"

"I didn't cheat on her." He slumped his shoulders. "At least not after I proposed to her."

"What? What do you mean?"

"Look, can I come inside? You're the only one who can help me fix this. She's not taking any of my calls."

"Fine," Amanda said through clenched teeth. Hex sniffed William, then trotted back into his bed near the couch. When she was close enough to William, she smacked him on the backside of his head.

"Ow!" he whined as he rubbed the spot where she'd hit him.

They sat down. "Explain."

"Okay." William sniffed, then said, "Caroline and I were seeing each other first. Back in high school, we dated each other off and on."

"I didn't know you guys dated back then," Amanda said, surprised.

"No one did. We didn't want to disrupt the friend group. Anyway, we would see each other during the summertime while in college. But then I ran into Rachel at a party, and that was when we decided to try dating."

"So, you were cheating on Caroline with Rachel?" Amanda asked, disgusted.

"No, not really. I never dated them at the same time. I'd see them interchangeably."

"That's just rich, Will. Just . . . wow."

"Look, don't judge me, okay? I'm just a guy. Both of them have great qualities. I just wish they were wrapped up into one girl. You know?"

"No, William, I don't know."

He slumped his shoulders. "Great. Now the only person who ever thought highly of me thinks the worst of me," he said, defeated.

"Why would it even matter what I think? It never mattered what I thought before, so why start worrying about it now? You knew how I felt about you for years and never cared to acknowledge me or my feelings. Why didn't you? Do you know how many times I tried to catch your attention? Do you know how many times I cried over you?" *Stop drudging up past feelings. None of this has anything to do with you. Get a grip!* Amanda chided herself. She took a deep breath, crossed her arms, then said, "Don't bother answering that. Just tell me why you were at Caroline's that day?"

He leaned his elbows on his knees, held his hands as if in prayer, and said, "I honestly thought Caroline invited us both over. I was expecting Rachel to be there when I got there. It turned out that Caroline wanted to talk to me alone. She wanted to have what she called *closure*. She wanted to know if I was sure I didn't want to marry her instead of Rachel. She knew Rachel was pregnant but was willing to overlook it if I wanted to marry her instead."

"She is so unbelievable. They're supposed to be best friends," Amanda said. "I don't get it."

"I don't either," William said. He rubbed the back of his neck. "I told her I should leave and that she should never ask me that question again. I told her we were over. Mandy, I love Rach." Amanda cringed from the use of the nickname she hated but didn't say anything. "You have to help me explain it to her. She's not gonna listen to me. You believe me, don't you? I never cheated on her. I'd never cheat on her." Tears streamed down his face.

She believed him. Amanda called Rachel. To her surprise, Rachel agreed to come over while William was there. Fifteen minutes later, Rachel was sitting in a chair in the kitchen while William was on his knees with his hands resting on each of Rachel's shoulders. He kept moving his head until she finally looked him in the eyes. He retold everything he had previously told Amanda to Rachel. "You mean it?" Rachel asked in a whisper, a tear rolling down her cheek. "You never cheated on me?"

William crossed his heart.

"You promise me you're over her and anyone else you may have played with?" she asked, her eyes full of hope.

"I promise you. My playing days have been over for a long time. I only want you and our kid, Rach."

She sniffed. "Okay."

They hugged and kissed.

On Saturday morning, Amanda woke to the ringing of her cell phone. She groggily answered to the sound of a panicked Rachel. "I'm sorry to do this to you," she said.

"What?" Amanda asked with a yawn, still half-asleep. She dreaded what new problem she'd be required to fix.

"Will you be my maid of honor? I'll pay you more if need be. I just don't know what else to do, and I don't have anyone I'd rather ask. You've been the one who's helped me the most, and I consider you a friend. You must think I'm pathetic, but oh, please, will you?"

Amanda sat up straight in her bed. Hex sprang to his feet and started doing circles in the bed. "Oh . . . I—"

"Caroline and I agreed that she should no longer come to the wedding, which means she won't be in it."

"Oh, right, of course. Why didn't I think of that? I'm the planner. I should have broached the subject," Amanda said.

"No, you've done so much that was out of the spectrum of your duties. This hasn't been your normal job by any means. Once again, I must apologize."

"It's okay, Rach. There's no need to keep apologizing to me, okay? I consider you a friend now too. We can be considered best friend–in-laws in some weird kinda way," Amanda joked.

Rachel laughed. "I guess you're right."

"But, yes, I'll be your maid of honor if you're sure that's what you want."

"Yes, please."

"Do you want me to wear Caroline's dress, or do you mind if I wear my own?" A part of her was proud of the fact that she and Caroline now wore the same dress size. In high school, that was not the case. There was some sort of victory in that knowledge.

"You decide. I just ask that it's red."

Her mother had talked her into buying a red dress when they went shopping. She usually avoided wearing the same color as the bridal party (especially red), but her mother insisted she make an exception for this wedding. "I'll wear my own. Thanks."

"I just have to call everyone and cancel tonight's bridal shower and bachelorette party. Honestly, I don't think Caroline organized anything," Rachel said softly.

"Oh, wait. No, don't do anything. Give me a couple of hours, and I'll call you back," Amanda said eagerly.

"Oh, okay," Rachel said hesitantly.

After disconnecting the call with Rachel, Amanda immediately dialed her brother's number. He picked up the phone after the first ring. "What's up, dork?" Matthew asked by way of greeting.

"Butthead, you have to help me out."

Matthew guffawed, then asked, "With what?"

"What were you planning for the bachelor party?"

She could hear and visualize her brother shrugging his shoulders as he said, "I dunno. Probably keep it simple. Beer, poker, and pizza."

"What happened to you?" Amanda said with a snort. "I totally called it. Listen. Let's combine the bachelor and bachelorette parties. Since Caroline's not in the wedding anymore I have to plan the bachelorette party. I seriously doubt she was planning anything anyway. I have an idea. I have a connection who can get us limos and drivers for cheap. You take the guys in one, and I'll take the girls in the other. We'll meet up at the new Mombo Room club in Palm Hills. That way, no one has to drive."

"You do remember Rachel is preggo, right?"

"All the more reason for her not to worry about driving. She can still dance. I happen to know she loves to dance, and so does Will. I think they'd prefer to do something together anyway."

"I agree."

"I'll announce it at the bridal shower tonight," Amanda said. "Rachel's mom insisted the shower be at her place. I think she didn't have much faith in Caroline either."

"They still have bridal showers?" Matthew asked.

"Yep, we could do that coed too, but let it go. You just handle getting the guys to meet up at your place, and I'll take care of handling the limos."

"Sounds good, sis. See you tonight."

The shower was as beautiful and luxurious as Rachel's mom's expectations warranted. The gifts were displayed. Finger foods, sparkling cider, and cupcakes were served, a few games were played with overpriced prizes handed out, and the party was over two hours after it had begun. Then the limo arrived. Except for Rachel's mom and aunts, all of the ladies piled into the car, and off they went to the Mombo Room in Palm Hills.

The building was three stories with a red-brick exterior and dark tinted windows. There were different dance floors and music on each floor. Music could be heard from the street. As soon as they entered, drinks were passed to them with a special nonalcoholic cherry martini for the bride. As soon as Dex saw Amanda, he scooped her up into an embrace, and with an enormous grin, he said, “This was a great idea. I’m horrible at poker.”

She laughed. She felt a flutter in her chest and excitement creep up from her tippy toes to her lips. She wanted to kiss Dex.

“Let’s dance,” he said as he led her to the dance floor, not waiting for her response. They danced the entire night, taking breaks only to grab an occasional drink.

Chapter Seventeen

It was two days before the wedding and the day of the rehearsal. “You’re fortunate your mom is who she is. Normally the church won’t allow weddings on Christmas Day,” one of the bridesmaids said to Rachel.

Amanda stood quietly to the side in the back of the church. They were waiting for the church’s appointed wedding planner to arrive. She could have easily instructed and guided everyone. She’d done plenty of weddings here at Saint Michael’s Catholic Church, but the church insisted they use their planner. Amanda was shocked to feel a sense of bitterness and jealousy rise up inside her. She hadn’t felt this way for a few weeks, yet it was bubbling up to the surface. It wasn’t fair to her other clients or anyone else who wanted to get married on Christmas. Just because Rachel’s mom had money and fame, it shouldn’t mean she could convince the church to do her bidding. She clenched her jaw when she glanced at the time on her cell phone and saw that the planner was nearly ten minutes late. “So unprofessional,” she grumbled.

“Are you okay?” Rachel asked. She placed a hand on Amanda’s shoulder.

Amanda shifted her eyes to the ceiling and then to Rachel's. "I should be asking you that. I apologize. The planner is late. I could start showing all of you what to expect if you'd like."

"That won't be necessary," a familiar high-pitched voice said with a slight southern accent. "Thank you, Amanda, for your patience, and to all of you. The real planner is here now. Let's get started, shall we?"

Amanda balled up her fist, took a deep breath, held it for a few seconds, and then blew it out slowly.

"You owe Amanda an apology. That was quite rude and inaccurate of you to say something like that," Rachel said to the woman.

"I agree," William said. His eyebrows furrowed. "She could have easily shown us all what to do. You've kept us waiting for an excessive amount of time. We could have run through it already."

The woman's face flushed. She cleared her throat, then turned to Amanda. "I apologize. That truly was a rude thing for me to say. Please forgive me."

Amanda wanted to roll her eyes but refrained. Instead, she said, "Forgiven."

"Great, thank you. Now let's begin," the woman directed.

During the rehearsal proceedings, Amanda kept observing Rachel and William's interaction. They looked at each other as if they shared the same soul and couldn't stand to be apart from one another. Their eyes seemed to shimmer when they made direct eye contact. It was annoying. Amanda felt herself getting crabbier and crabbier by the second. She just wanted to go home. Yet, she was expected to follow everyone to Paul's Italian Pizzeria for dinner immediately after this.

"I hope you don't mind, but I told Dex to meet us at the restaurant," Matt whispered as the planner lined everyone up to practice leaving the church after the ceremony. Since he was the best man, he walked with Amanda while his wife walked with Rachel's cousin. Amanda still wondered if it was right for her to be the maid of honor instead of Kimberly. But she'd honor Rachel's request.

"Thanks, bro," Amanda said as she looped her arm around her brother's. At least she wouldn't have to sit alone while everyone was coupled up at dinner.

"You hangin' in there?" Matt asked, concern evident in his voice and expression.

"Of course. I'm happy for them. They make a beautiful couple."

"You sure? Because the way you were glaring at them a few minutes ago, it doesn't seem like it."

"Rachel is one of my closest friends now. I'm her maid of honor, for crying out loud," Amanda said in a harsh whisper.

"So was Caroline, and we know what happened there."

"Don't you dare compare me to her!" Amanda roared. She could suddenly feel all eyes on her.

"Everything okay there?" the planner asked.

"Yes," Matt said.

"Good, keep moving. We're almost done."

When the rehearsal was finally over, Matt asked her, "So you'll be at Mom and Dad's tomorrow for Christmas Eve dinner?"

"Of course," Amanda snapped.

Matt held his hands up in surrender. "Okay, message received. I'll leave you alone. It would be best to get your attitude in check," he warned with a glare.

Amanda's scowl deepened.

The entire bridal party met at Paul's Italian Pizzeria for dinner less than an hour later. Dex was waiting at the reserved table when

Amanda arrived. He could see she was crabby from the expression on her face.

"Hey, Manz," Dex greeted with a smile. He hoped some of his cheer would rub off on her.

"Hi," she said as she sat next to him.

William and Rachel giggled as they whispered something to each other at the far right of the table. Amanda grunted.

"You seem a bit prickly tonight," Dex said. He watched her as she studied Will and Rachel. "You okay?"

Amanda shrugged her shoulders.

Dex reached for her hand as he rose to his feet. He pulled her up and said, "Let's get some fresh air and chat outside."

She frowned but did as he suggested. He continued to hold her hand as they walked. When they were out on the restaurant's deserted patio, they faced each other and Dex said, "Spill it. What's got you so cranky tonight? I thought you were okay with their wedding?"

It was brisk. A cool breeze brushed past them, and she shivered. Dex took off his jacket and placed it over her shoulders. He reached for her hands again and waited. She swallowed, coughed, shifted from foot to foot, then sniffed. Finally, she said, "I don't know. I am. I mean—" She sniffed again. "I am happy for them. I'm thankful they chose me to plan their wedding, and I'm happy that I made a new friend out of Rachel. But . . ." She paused as her eyes watered, and she mustered up the courage to admit the truth. "I'm jealous."

Dex felt as if someone was squeezing his heart, and Amanda was the only one who could stop it. He felt himself pale. *How could she still have a crush on William?* He released her hands. "Why?"

She looked up at the nighttime sky. Amanda chewed on her bottom lip briefly, then said, "They have it all. They're about to have a baby. They have great careers, and just look how they were inside. I'm alone. I bust my butt, and for what? Just to be called a kid and be treated as if I'm an idiot daily."

"What? Where is this coming from?" Dex asked.

"I don't even know. Just at the rehearsal, I could feel myself getting so angry. The church that I go to won't even acknowledge me as a serious event planner. Why is that? Sure, I don't go to Mass the way I should, but they know me. They know who I am and what I do. They still insist on my clients using their wedding planners. Then I just started getting furious because normally no one is permitted to get married on Christmas. But just because Rachel's mom is famous and has money to give away, they made an exception. I felt small. I'm tired of everyone viewing me as a kid and not taking me seriously."

Her light-brown eyes glistened with unshed tears. Dex's heartbeat increased as he grabbed her hands and tugged her close to him.

"I just—" she started, but before she could finish her sentence, he kissed her. His heart thudded in his chest. Time slowed. The sounds around them ceased. Dex could smell her coconut shampoo and conditioner. He could taste the watermelon lip gloss she must have recently put on. He felt the softness of her lips and could sense the moment she caught her breath from surprise. Then Dex felt her lean into him, relaxed, as if she melted in his arms. She opened her mouth for him, inviting him to explore her. Their tongues danced the most perfect dance of his life. He'd given her his heart the moment she moved next door. He was hers.

When their lips finally parted, their foreheads touched. Dex said, "I know more than anyone you're not a kid."

"Can we"—she wasn't looking at him but at her feet when she paused, then continued—"do that again?"

He gently lifted her chin with his right hand to look into her eyes. "Absolutely." Then he kissed her again.

He wished they were at home, either one of their homes, instead of a restaurant. Dex didn't want to go back inside. He wanted to explore more of her, but eventually, she pulled slowly away from him. "Um," she whispered, looking into his eyes again. "Thank you for that. We should get back inside." She turned and walked away.

Chapter Eighteen

It was Christmas Eve, the day before the wedding. Dex was left frustrated and flustered after the kiss last night. Once they had re-entered the restaurant, Amanda avoided contact with him even though they sat next to each other. It was as if she wanted to pretend the kiss never happened.

Although, he'd noticed she was no longer crabby. She was flushed the rest of the night and talked to everyone, laughed and joked but didn't say a word to him. She didn't even ask him what his plans were for today. For the past few years, they had Christmas Eve breakfast together. Then in the evening and the following day, they'd each go to their respective family gatherings. He had hoped to spend some time with her today, but there were no messages. No sign that the kisses happened. Was it all in his mind? Were the feelings he felt one-sided? What if he'd just demolished his friendship with her? What if she suddenly wanted nothing to do with him? What was he supposed to do?

"You were supposed to wait for her to make the first move!" he shouted to himself. "She was supposed to tell you how she feels before the wedding." He smacked his forehead a few times with the palm of his right hand. "Stupid, stupid, stupid."

Amanda had a few last-minute errands to run on behalf of William and Rachel. She needed to check with the hotel to ensure everything was ready for tomorrow, along with the bakery and Jasmine's band. Amanda was confident her brother would make certain the photographer from his studio was ready, so she didn't worry about that. She didn't have much time to overthink the amazing kisses with Dex. It lingered in the back of her mind and was imprinted permanently on her heart. She was also expected to be at her parents' house for dinner, midnight Mass, and their gift exchange. She thought of texting Dex but didn't want to cause unnecessary pressure on him. She was sure he kissed her to calm her down and help her off the ledge she was on. She wished it was a kiss that meant her feelings for him were reciprocated. But there was no way he wanted to date her. He had called her *kid* too many times in the past. It was a sympathy kiss, or rather kisses. "Stop thinking about it," she told herself as she backed out of her driveway that morning. "Focus. You have too much to do today."

Once all of her wedding errands were done, Amanda realized she still had a few more gifts to buy before heading to her parents' house. She thought of calling Dex to see if he would want to tag along with her, but she wasn't sure she was ready to face him. She knew they would need to talk. "Nope, not right now." They could speak tomorrow after the wedding.

When she arrived at her parents' house later that evening, she was bombarded with hugs and eggnog. "Drink this before the kids ask you for any," Kimberly said. "This is the adults-only stash."

"I don't like eggnog," Amanda said. She tried to hand the mug back to Kimberly, but it was shoved back to her.

"Chug it, hurry," Kimberly said.

"You're so bossy," Amanda said.

"Do it!" Kimberly urged, nudging the cup to Amanda's lips, threatening to pour it down her throat.

Amanda chugged it, then coughed. "Was there any eggnog in there?"

Kimberly cackled. "Just a little bit."

"We have a busy day tomorrow, so don't go overboard with the drinking," Amanda said.

"Bah, that's what painkillers and coffee are for."

"Auntie!" Lexi shouted before enveloping her in a tight hug. "I haven't seen you in forever."

"It's been a little over a week," Amanda said, laughing.

"Can I spend the night at your house at some point this week? My brother keeps screaming in the middle of the night. I haven't been able to sleep for the past few days."

"He's just doing his job, Lexi. He's only a few months old."

"It doesn't mean I should lose sleep over it."

"Of course, you can spend the night," Amanda finally answered.

"Thank you! And can we do tie-dye shirts? Mom won't let me. She says it's too messy."

"Absolutely. That's what I'm here for," Amanda said.

"You're welcome to take the baby anytime too, you know." Matthew said. He was sipping on a large mug of eggnog. "Where's Dex?"

"At his sister's, I'm guessing," Amanda said with a shrug.

Matt tilted his head and asked, "What's going on with you two?"

"What do you mean?"

"You barely spoke to him last night. Did you two fight?"

"No, of course not. Just busy with the wedding stuff," Amanda said.

"Liar. Something happened last night. You two usually have your own private party at gatherings, but you seemed to be avoiding him."

"We were eating at a restaurant. What do you expect?"

"Why are you lying to your own brother?" Matt asked.

"What's going on with you?" Monica asked Dex. They were relaxing on the couch in front of the Christmas tree while her kids played video games. "You've been mopey ever since you got here. Usually, you're annoyingly cheerful and singing Christmas carols obnoxiously with the kids. What's up?" She took a sip of the red wine she'd been drinking.

Dex snorted and said, "I'm perfectly cheerful. I'm happy."

"Lies," Monica said. "Does this have something to do with Amanda?"

He felt himself blush and said, "Nope. Nothing is wrong."

"Where is she? I thought you two would be hanging out today."

"We usually do our own thing on Christmas Eve, thank you very much. She's probably at her parents' house."

"Probably?" Monica asked curiously. "Why don't you know?"

"Good grief. I'm not her warden. We're neighbors. That's it."

"You're an idiot," Monica said.

Yes, I am, Dex thought, but would never admit it to his sister.

"Is everything ready for the wedding tomorrow?"

"I guess."

"There you go again with the guessing. Why don't you know for sure?"

"Because she's avoiding me, okay?" He finally burst.

"What? Why?" Monica asked. She placed her wineglass on the maple coffee table.

Dex's shoulders slumped as he confessed, "I kissed her last night."

Monica grinned. "Finally! That's great!"

He shook his head. "No, it's not. She doesn't want anything to do with me now. Manz avoided me the rest of the night after that. She hasn't called me or texted me. We usually have breakfast on Christmas Eve, but we didn't."

"Did you think of reaching out to her? You know she's probably busy. The wedding is tomorrow."

"I don't want to bother her." Dex pouted.

Monica nudged him on the shoulder. "You wouldn't be bothering her. You'd be showing her you care, and that you don't regret kissing her."

"I do regret kissing her. She was ranting and raving about the wedding, and she looked so hurt and lost that the only thing I could think of doing was kissing her. I shouldn't have done that."

"Did she tell you she didn't want to kiss you? Did she kiss you back?"

"No, yes. I mean, Amanda kissed me back. But it was just a moment. After that, she didn't want me around. I think I'm going to skip the wedding. I have no business there."

"The bride and the groom invited you, and didn't Amanda's brother invite you too?"

"Right, everyone except for Amanda," Dex said pathetically.

"But you're always her plus-one. You're automatically included!" Monica smacked him on the back of his head.

He sniffed, then said, “Nope, not going.”

Monica huffed.

Chapter Nineteen

On Christmas Day, it was warm and sunny with clear blue skies. The ladies were getting ready in a reserved room at the church. Everything else was running smoothly except for the cake being accidentally delivered to the church hall instead of the hotel. Amanda had just finished checking on last-minute details a few minutes before the ceremony when her mom stopped her. "Amanda, here." Her mom handed her a tube of lipstick. "Put this on, then get to the back of the church. You need to get out of planner mode and into maid-of-honor mode."

Amanda hugged her. "Thanks, Mom."

"You're doing great. Everything is looking great. Now just breathe and take a moment to calm your nerves. You've got this," Amanda's mom said encouragingly. "I'm proud of you."

Amanda allowed her mother's words to wash over her. She wanted to cry. It meant so much to her.

"No crying," her mom said as if reading her mind. "No time to fix your makeup. Now go." Her mom nudged her toward the church entrance, where the other bridesmaids waited. Rachel hid in a cubby near the opening, away from wedding guests. Rachel's uncle, who was giving her away, was standing close by, deterring anyone from approaching her. The uncle waved to Amanda. Amanda gave him a thumbs-up. He returned the signal. They were ready to begin. Amanda signaled for the music to start inside the church.

The ceremony was a blur of action and motion. Until she was walking out of the church, Amanda realized she hadn't seen Dex anywhere. She didn't have time to question it. She assumed they'd meet each other at the reception at some point. There was more fuzziness as the ritual of moving from the ceremony, to photos, to the reception, and everything in between went on. She hadn't eaten all day except for a few bites of a bagel and coffee. It was now almost four o'clock in the afternoon. Jasmine had agreed to make the needed announcements between sets.

After all the guests were seated and dinner had been served, Amanda finally had a moment to breathe. She was sitting at the wedding party table and glanced around the hall. It was magical. There was a beautifully decorated Christmas tree in each corner of the room. White twinkling lights were strung around the walls, along with red, gold, and silver ribbons. Kids were running around playing tag. She had to intervene a few times to stop them from tumbling into someone or something but other guests were now monitoring them. The guests appeared to be enjoying themselves. Amanda gave herself credit for a job well done. But she felt uneasiness in her heart. Where was Dex? Her eyes skimmed over each of the tables.

"I don't see him anywhere," Kimberly said, reading her mind. She was sitting next to Amanda. "Maybe you should call him."

"He would have come if he'd wanted to. I can't force him to be here if he doesn't want to be," Amanda said.

"He's not a mind reader, Amanda. What happened? You two are always together."

"Nothing," Amanda denied.

"Be honest," Kimberly urged. Just then, Amanda's stomach growled. "And eat," she added.

Amanda cut up her chicken breast, took a bite, and then scooped up potatoes.

"So, tell me what happened," Kimberly pressed.

"Fine," Amanda said before taking a sip of water. She swallowed and then admitted, "We kissed the other day. The night of the rehearsal. But it was a sympathy kiss. When we were out on the patio, I kind of lost my wits and started venting about stuff and—"

She rubbed her face, but Kimberly smacked her hand, preventing her from rubbing any further.

"You'll ruin your makeup. We still have a few more photos to take," Kimberly interrupted.

Amanda grunted.

"Wait a minute! You kissed!" Kimberly shouted.

"Keep your voice down," Amanda whispered.

"But you kissed! You finally did it!" Kimberly bounced excitedly in her seat.

"You're not listening. It was a sympathy kiss."

"There's no such thing as a sympathy kiss, Amanda!" Kimberly thundered.

"Will you please keep your voice down?" Amanda pleaded.

"He should be here," Kimberly said. "Oh no, I'm not having it! We've all waited far too long for this kiss to happen!" Before Amanda could stop her, Kimberly rose to her feet, walked over to the groomsmen side of the long table, and chatted with Matthew. Rachel and William were also pulled into whatever conversation they were having.

"It's about time!" William shouted.

Even though Amanda was sitting next to Rachel, she couldn't hear any of the other words the four were whispering. The group was taking turns peeking over and glancing at Amanda.

"What?" Amanda asked. She could feel her mood turning sour.

"Don't stress over it," Matthew finally announced. He pointed a thumb to himself. "I'll handle it."

"You go, baby!" Kimberly cheered.

"What?" Amanda asked worriedly.

"Oh, you just hush and don't worry about it," Kimberly said as she made her way back to her seat. "Finish eating."

"So bossy," Amanda said, but she did as she was told while still worrying about what the group was plotting against her.

Amanda noticed after the first dance was announced that her brother had disappeared.

Dex had just finished yard work in the front of his house when a gray Toyota Corolla pulled up in his driveway. A man with a tuxedo stepped out of the car, wearing a menacing scowl on his face.

It took Dex a moment to realize the man was Amanda's brother. He dropped the hose he'd been holding and took a guarded step back.

"Get dressed, now, and let's go."

Dex blinked, not understanding the words.

"What are you doing?" Matthew asked.

Dex raised his hands as if in surrender. "Yard work."

"You should be at the wedding dancing with my sister. What are you thinking?"

"I— I— I don't know."

"Obviously. Take the fastest shower of your life, get dressed, and get in the car."

"But—" Dex started.

"Do you love my sister or not?" Matthew asked.

"Yes, but—"

Matt pointed to Dex's front door. "Shower now."

Dex nodded, turned, and went into the house.

Amanda was sitting at the bridal table, fidgeting with the dessert fork. She had only taken a bite or two of the ordinarily scrumptious cake. She heard Rachel's laughter for the millionth time. Amanda peered up to see the bride dancing with two kids. Rachel was the poster of all that a bride should be. From the corner of her eye, she saw movement at the hall entrance. Amanda turned and saw her brother with his right hand around the back of Dex's neck. Her eyes widened in disbelief as she witnessed her brother pointing to where she was sitting and him shoving Dex farther into the hall.

Dex stumbled briefly but regained his balance, straightened his tie, and walked toward her.

"Hi," Amanda said when he finally sat next to her, taking Kimberly's seat.

"Hi," he said. "That was humiliating."

"I'm sorry my brother did that to you," she said.

"I deserved it," he said.

"No, you didn't," Amanda said.

"I'm sorry. I shouldn't have kissed you the other night," Dex said.

Amanda's shoulders sagged, and she frowned. "Oh."

He reached for her hand. "That's not entirely accurate, Manz." He turned his chair. He released her hand to maneuver her chair so that they could face each other. Then Dex grabbed each of her hands. "I've been an idiot for a long time now."

She swallowed.

"The truth is I'm in love with you, Manz. I don't want to be just friends anymore. I want more. I want to kiss you, make love. I want to know every single part of you."

Her eyes lit up from surprise and then happiness. “I’m in love with you too,” she whispered.

He grinned the goofiest grin she’d ever seen him wear, which caused her to smile.

He leaned in, and so did she. They kissed.

Chapter Twenty

Amanda had gained five new clients due to Rachel and William's wedding, two of which were celebrities. She would be busy for the next year and not have to work other jobs for the first time since starting her business. She may have to consider hiring additional help. Dex had spent each day with her since the wedding. It was now New Year's Eve, and they were at a beach party for one of Dex's clients. They had just finished dancing when Dex tugged her away. "Let's go for a stroll."

"Okay," she said.

Dex grabbed two flutes filled with champagne and gestured with his head to walk toward the waves. Amanda reached for one of the flutes and then held his free hand. They each took a sip.

"I normally don't like champagne, but it tastes outstanding tonight," Dex said.

"I agree," Amanda said.

They each removed their shoes and walked barefoot as they got closer to the shoreline. "It's nice out," Dex said. Amanda wasn't sure if she imagined it, but Dex's voice sounded a bit jittery, as if he were nervous about something. He looked up at the sky. "We can see the stars tonight."

Amanda took a sip and peered up at the sky too. "Oh," she gasped, "it's beautiful." A cool, gentle breeze brushed up against them. She closed her eyes. "This is nice."

Dex surprised her with a kiss. When their lips broke apart, he said, "I want to do this right." He tugged her back to dry sand, then knelt on one knee. "Manz, I want to start the new year off as your fiancé. I want us to start practicing making babies. I want us to start figuring out whose house we're going to live in or if we buy a new one. I want us to start picking out furniture and going to Home Depot together."

"We already pick out furniture together and go to Home Depot," she teased.

"You know what I mean," Dex said as he pulled out a blue velvet box from his pants pocket.

She tried not to gasp but failed. "No, I don't," Amanda said. "You haven't asked me anything yet." She swallowed.

"Amanda Alexander, will you marry me and make beautiful babies together?" Dex asked. His eyes glimmered.

She knelt in front of him and said, "Yes!" Then she tackled him with kisses into the sand.

~*~*~*~

If you enjoyed reading this novella, please leave a review on Amazon.com or Goodreads.com.

More books by Giselle Lumas

Romance:

Captain of My Heart

The Captain's Son

Alida's Way

Truth or Dare: A Love Story

A Holiday Bet

Tug of Love

Melody's Blues

Sandy Times

Forty Weeks to You

The Twelve Years of Christmas

The Captain's Love: The Complete Two-Part Series

Science Fiction/Fantasy:

Her Forgotten Halo

Malique's Quest

Lani's Mission (The World Through a Shaded Eye: Book One)

Cozy Mystery:

Spilling the Jelly Beans (Beach City Cozy Mysteries: Patsy - Book One)

Santa's Helper Bytes the Dust (Beach City Cozy Mysteries: Patsy - Book Two)

Nailed It! (Beach City Cozy Mysteries: Patsy - Book Three)

Teen:

Journal of a Cymbal Player

Children's:

The Superhero Who Saved Christmas

www.ingramcontent.com/pod-product-compliance
Lightning Source LLC
LaVergne TN
LVHW010605160826
845677LV00013B/3250

* 9 7 9 8 8 3 8 8 9 0 3 8 2 *